Who Killed Palomino Molero?

BOOKS BY MARIO VARGAS LLOSA

The Cubs and Other Stories

The Time of the Hero

The Green House

Captain Pantoja and the Special Service

Conversation in the Cathedral

Aunt Julia and the Scriptwriter

The War of the End of the World

The Real Life of Alejandro Mayta

The Perpetual Orgy

Who Killed Palomino Molero?

Who Killed
Palomino Molero?

MARIO VARGAS LLOSA

Translated by Alfred Mac Adam

Collier Books
Macmillan Publishing Company
New York

Collier Books
Macmillan Publishing Company
866 Third Avenue, New York, NY 10022
Collier Macmillan Canada, Inc.

Library of Congress Cataloging-in-Publication Data

Vargas Llosa, Mario, 1936–
    Who killed Palomino Molero?

    Translation of: ¿Quién mató a Palomino Molero?
    I. Title.
[PQ8498.32.A65Q513   1988]   863   87-32015
ISBN 0-02-022570-9

Cover illustration © by John Jinks

Cover design by Lee Wade

First Collier Books Edition 1988

10 9 8 7 6 5 4 3 2 1

Printed in the United States of America

To José Miguel Oviedo

Who Killed Palomino Molero?

1

"SONS OF BITCHES." Lituma felt the vomit rising in his throat. "Kid, they really did a job on you."

The boy had been both hung and impaled on the old carob tree. His position was so absurd that he looked more like a scarecrow or a broken marionette than a corpse. Before or after they killed him, they slashed him to ribbons: his nose and mouth were split open; his face was a crazy map of dried blood, bruises, cuts, and cigarette burns. Lituma saw they'd even tried to castrate him; his testicles hung down to his thighs. He was barefoot, naked from the waist down, with a ripped T-shirt covering his upper body. He was young, thin, dark, and bony. Under the labyrinth of flies buzzing around his face, his hair glistened, black and curly.

The goats belonging to the boy who'd found the body were nosing around, scratching around the field looking for something to eat. Lituma thought they might begin to gnaw on the dead man's feet at any moment.

"Who the fuck did this?" he stammered, holding back his gorge.

"I don't know," said the boy. "Don't get mad at me, it's not my fault. You should be glad I told you about it."

"I'm not mad at you. I'm mad that anybody could be bastard enough to do something like this."

The boy must have had the shock of his life this morning when he drove his goats over the rocky field and stumbled onto this horror. But he did his duty: he left his herd browsing among the rocks around the corpse and ran to the police station in Talara. Which was quite a feat because Talara was a good hour's walk from the pasture. Lituma remembered his sweaty face and his scared voice when he walked through the station-house door:

"They killed a guy over on the road to Lobitos. I can take you there if you want, but we have to go now because I left my goats all alone and somebody could steal them."

Luckily, no goats were stolen. As he was getting over the jolt of seeing the body, Lituma had noticed the boy counting his goats on his fingers. He heard him breathe a sigh of relief: "All here."

"Holy Mother of God!" exclaimed the taxi driver. "What the hell is this?"

On the way, the boy had described, more or less, what they were going to see, but it was one thing to imagine it and quite another to see it and smell it. The corpse stank to high heaven. The sun was boring holes through the rocks and through their very skulls. He must have been rotting at a record pace.

"Will you help me get him down, buddy?"

"Why not?" grunted the taxi driver, crossing himself. He spit at the carob tree. "If someone had told me what the Ford was going to be carrying, I'd never of bought it. You and the lieutenant take advantage of me because I'm such a nice guy."

Jerónimo had the only taxi in Talara. His old van, as big and black as a hearse, passed freely through the gate that separated the town from the zone where the foreigners who were employed by the International Petroleum Company lived and worked. Lieutenant Silva and Lituma used the taxi whenever they had to go anywhere too far to use horses or bicycles—the only transport available at the Guardia Civil post. The driver moaned and complained every time they called him, saying they made him lose money, despite the fact that the lieutenant always paid for the gasoline himself.

"Wait, Jerónimo, I just remembered we can't touch him until the judge comes and holds his inquest."

"Which means I'll be making this little trip again," croaked the old man. "Either the judge pays me or you find another sucker."

Just then, he tapped himself on the forehead, opened his eyes wide, and looked the corpse in the face. "Wait a minute! I know this guy!"

"Who is he?"

"One of the boys they brought to the air base among the last bunch of recruits." The old man's face lit up. "That's right. The guy from Piura who sang boleros."

2

"HE SANG BOLEROS? Then he's got to be the guy I told you about," Mono said again.

"He is. We checked; he's the same guy. Palomino Molero, from Castilla. But that doesn't tell us who killed him."

They were near the stadium in La Chunga's little bar. There must have been a prizefight in progress because they could hear the shouts of the fans. Lituma had come to Piura on his day off; a truck driver from the I.P.C. brought him that morning and was going back to Talara at midnight. Whenever he came to Piura, Lituma went on the town with his cousins, José and Mono León, and with Josefino, a friend from the Gallinacera neighborhood. Lituma and the León brothers were from La Mangachería, but the long-standing rivalry between the two neighborhoods meant nothing to the four friends. They were so close they'd written their own theme song and called themselves the Unstoppables.

"Figure this one out and they'll make you a general, Lituma," wisecracked Mono.

"It's going to be tough. Nobody knows anything, nobody

saw anything, and the worst part is that the authorities won't lift a finger to help."

"Wait a minute, aren't you the authorities over in Talara?" asked Josefino, genuinely surprised.

"Lieutenant Silva and I are the police authority. The authority I'm talking about is the Air Force. That skinny kid was in the Air Force, so if they don't help us, who the fuck will?"

Lituma blew the foam off his beer and took a swallow, opening his mouth like a crocodile. "Motherfuckers. If you guys had seen what they did to the kid, you wouldn't be grinning your way down to the whorehouse like this. You'd understand why I can't think about anything else."

"We do understand," said Josefino. "But talking about a corpse all the time is boring. Why don't you forget about the guy, Lituma? He's dead."

"That's what you get for becoming a cop," said José. "Work is a disease. Besides, you're no good at that stuff. A cop should have a heart made of stone, because he has to be a motherfucker sometimes. And you're so damn sentimental."

"It's true, I am. I just can't stop thinking about that skinny kid. I have nightmares, I think someone's pulling off my balls the way they did to him. His balls were hanging down to his knees, smashed as flat as a pair of fried eggs."

"Did you touch them?" Mono asked, laughing.

"Talk about eggs and balls, did Lieutenant Silva screw that fat woman yet?" José asked.

"We've been on pins and needles ever since you told us about it," added Josefino. "Did he screw her or not?"

"At the rate he's going, he'll never screw her."

José got up from the table. "Okay, let's go to the movies. Before midnight the whorehouse is like a funeral parlor. They're showing a cowboy film at the Variety with Rosita Quintana. The cop's treating, of course."

"Me? I don't even have the dough for this beer. You'll let me pay later, won't you, Chunguita?"

"Maybe your mama will let you pay later," answered La Chunga, looking bored.

"I figured you'd say something like that. I just wanted to screw around."

"Go screw around with your mama."

"Two points for La Chunga; zero for Lituma," Mono announced. "La Chunga wins."

"Don't get steamed, Chunguita. Here's what I owe you. And lay off my mom: she's dead and buried over in Simbilá."

La Chunga, a tall, sour woman of uncertain age, snatched up the money, counted it, and gave back the change as the Unstoppables were leaving.

"One question, Chunguita. Didn't anyone ever crack a bottle over your head for being such a wise guy?"

"Since when have you been so curious," she replied, not deigning to look at him.

"Someday someone's going to give you a lesson in good manners."

"I'll bet it won't be you," said La Chunga, yawning.

The four Unstoppables walked along the sandy path that led to the main road, passed the Piura blueblood club, and headed toward Grau's monument. It was a warm night, quiet and starry. The mixed smells of carob trees, goats, birdshit, and deep frying filled the air. Lituma, unable to erase from his mind the picture of the impaled and bloody Palomino Molero, wondered if he'd be sorry he'd become a cop instead of living the free and easy life of the Unstoppables. No, he wouldn't be sorry. Even though work was a bitch, he ate every day, and his life was free of uncertainties. José, Mono, and Josefino were whistling a waltz in counterpoint, and Lituma was trying to imagine the lulling tones and the "captivating melodies" of the kid's boleros. At the entrance to the Variety, he said goodbye to his cousins and Josefino. He lied to them, saying the truck driver from the International was going back to Talara earlier than usual and that he didn't want to miss his ride. They tried to shake him down for some cash, but he didn't give them a cent.

He headed for the Plaza de Armas. On the way he spotted the poet Joaquín Ramos on the corner, wearing a monocle and pulling along the goat he called his gazelle. The plaza was crowded, as if people were there for some church function. Lituma paid no attention to them and, making as if he were going to meet a woman, crossed the Old Bridge over to Castilla. The idea had taken shape while he was drinking his beer in La Chunga's. Suppose she wasn't there? What if she'd moved to some other city to put her grief behind her?

But there she was, sitting on a bench in the doorway of her house, enjoying the cool of the evening as she shucked some corn. Through the open door of the adobe hut, Lituma could see the woman's few pieces of furniture:

cane chairs (some without seats), a table, some clay
pitchers, a box she used as a dresser, and a tinted photograph. "The kid," he thought.

"Evening." He stood in front of the woman. She was
barefoot, wearing the same black dress she had on that
morning in the Talara Police Station.

"Evening," she murmured, looking at him without recognizing him. Some squalid dogs sniffed at him and growled.
In the distance, someone strummed a guitar.

"May I talk with you for a minute, Doña Asunta? About
your son Palomino."

In the half light, Lituma could just make out her furrowed, wrinkled face, her tiny eyes covered by puffy lids
scrutinizing him uneasily. Were her eyes always like that,
or were they swollen from crying?

"Don't you recognize me? I'm Officer Lituma, from
Talara. I was there when Lieutenant Silva took your
statement."

She crossed herself, muttered something incomprehensible, and Lituma watched her laboriously stand up. She
went into the house, carrying her corn and her bench. He
followed her and took off his cap as soon as he was inside.
He was moved by the fact that this had been Palomino
Molero's house. He was not following orders but his own
initiative; he hoped it wouldn't mean trouble.

"Did you find it?" she mumbled in the same tremulous
voice she used in Talara to make her declaration. She
sagged into a chair, and since Lituma stared at her ques-
tioningly, she raised her voice. "My son's guitar. Did you
find it?"

"Not yet." He remembered Doña Asunta sobbing as she answered Lieutenant Silva's questions, and constantly asking about getting back Palomino's guitar. But after she'd gone, neither he nor the lieutenant remembered. "Don't worry. Sooner or later it'll turn up, and I'll bring it to you myself."

She crossed herself again, and it seemed to Lituma she was exorcising him. "I bring it all back to her."

"He wanted to leave it here, but I told him, Bring it with you, bring it with you. No, Ma, at the base I won't have any time to play. Besides, I might not even have a locker to store it in. Let it stay here. I'll play when I come to Piura. No, Palomino, take it with you so you can pass the time better, so you can accompany yourself when you sing. Don't give up your guitar when you love it so much. Oh, God . . . my poor child."

She started to cry, and Lituma was sorry he'd stirred up the old woman's memories. He muttered some broken consolations as he scratched his neck. He sat down, just to do something. Yes, the photograph was of Palomino making his First Communion. For a long time, Lituma stared at the long, angular little face of the dark-skinned boy with his hair slicked down, dressed all in white, with a candle in his right hand, a missal in his left, and a scapulary around his neck. The photographer had reddened his cheeks and lips. A scrawny kid, in a rapture, as if he were contemplating the infant Jesus.

"Already he sang beautifully," whimpered Doña Asunta, pointing to the photo. "Father García had him sing by himself, and everybody clapped, right during Mass."

"Everybody said he had a terrific voice. He might have become an artist, like the ones that sing on the radio and make tours. Everybody says so. Artists shouldn't get drafted. They should be exempt."

"Palomino didn't get drafted. He was exempt."

Lituma looked her in the eye. The old lady crossed herself and started to cry again. As he listened to her crying, Lituma stared at the insects swarming around the lamp. There were dozens, buzzing and crashing again and again into the glass shade, trying to reach the flame. They wanted to kill themselves, the idiots.

"The fortune-teller said that when the guitar is found the murderers will be found, too. Whoever's got his guitar killed him. Murderers! Murderers!"

Lituma nodded in agreement. He was dying for a smoke, but to light up a cigarette in the presence of this grieving lady seemed sacrilegious to him.

"Your son was exempt from military service?"

"The only son of a widow," recited Doña Asunta. "Palomino was the last; the other two died. That's the law."

"It's true, so many unfair things happen." Lituma scratched his neck once again, certain she was going to start crying again. "I mean, they had no right to call him up, right? You call that justice? If he hadn't been drafted, he'd be alive. For sure."

Doña Asunta shook her head as she dried her eyes on the hem of her dress. In the distance they could still hear the guitars, and Lituma suddenly fantasized that the guy playing out there in the darkness, maybe on the riverbank watching the moon, was Palomino.

"They didn't draft him; he enlisted." Doña Asunta was

still weeping. "Nobody made him go. He went into the Air Force because he wanted to. He brought on his own tragedy."

Lituma stood there, silently watching the seated woman, who was so short her bare feet scarcely reached the floor.

"He took the bus to Talara, went into the base, and said he wanted to join up. Poor baby! He was going to his death. He did it himself. My poor Palomino!"

"Why didn't you tell this to Lieutenant Silva when you were in Talara?"

"He never asked. I answered every question he asked me."

That was true. Did Palomino have any enemies? Did anyone ever threaten him? Had she ever heard of his arguing or fighting with someone? Did anyone have any reason to harm him? Had he told her he was thinking of deserting? Asunta meekly answered every question: no, nobody, never. But the truth was that the lieutenant had never thought of asking if the kid had been drafted or if he enlisted.

"You mean he liked being in the service?" Lituma was shocked: the impression he had of the bolero singer was completely false.

"That's the part I don't understand," she wailed. "Why did you do it, Palomino? You, in the Air Force? You? You? In Talara? Planes crash; do you want to scare me to death? How could you do it without talking to me first? Because if I did, you'd have said no, Mama. But why, Palomino? Because I have to go to Talara. Because it's a matter of of life and death, Mama."

"And why was it a life-and-death matter for your son to go to Talara?"

"I never found out." She crossed herself for the fourth or fifth time. "He wouldn't tell me and he's taken his secret to the grave. Oh! Why did you do this to me, Palomino?"

A brown goat with white spots poked its head into the room and stared at the woman with its big, pitying eyes. A shadow pulled it away.

"He must have been sorry as soon as he joined. When he discovered that military life is not fun, games, and girls but a lot of drill, spit, and polish. That's probably why he deserted. That much I can understand. What I don't get is why they killed him. And in such a cruel way."

He'd been thinking out loud, but Doña Asunta didn't seem to notice. So he enlisted to get out of Piura, because it was a matter of life and death. Someone must have threatened him here in town and he thought he'd be safe in Talara, on the Air Force base. But he couldn't take military life, so he deserted. The person or persons he ran away from found him and killed him. But why like that? You've got to be crazy to torture someone who's still just a kid. Lots of guys join up because their love life has fallen apart. Maybe he was turned down. Maybe he was in love and the girl gave him a hard time, or cheated on him. He got bitter and decided to get away. Where? Talara. How? By enlisting. It seemed believable and unbelievable all at the same time. He nervously scratched his neck again.

"Why have you come to my house?" Doña Asunta suddenly turned toward him.

He felt he'd been caught in a lie. Why had he come? No good reason, unhealthy curiosity.

"To find out if you could give me any clues," he stuttered.

Doña Asunta's disgust showed in her eyes, and Lituma thought she knew he was lying.

"You had me over there for three hours telling you all I know," she whispered, grieving. "What more do you want? What more? Do you think I know who killed my son?"

"Don't get mad. I don't want to upset you, so I'll be on my way. Thanks for talking to me. We'll get in touch with you if we find out anything."

He got up, said good night, and went out without shaking hands with her, afraid she wouldn't take his hand. Outside, he stuck his cap on his head and calmed down after walking a few steps down the dirt road, under the glittering stars. The distant guitar had fallen silent. All he could hear were the shrill voices of children fighting or playing, the chatter of the adults in front of their houses, and some dogs barking. What's wrong with you? he thought. What's gotten into you? The poor kid. He couldn't be the easygoing guy from La Mangachería again until he understood how there could be people in the world that evil. Especially because everybody was saying that Palomino wouldn't hurt a fly.

Lituma reached the Old Bridge, but instead of crossing over to the city, he went into the Río Bar, which was built on the ancient bridge over the Piura River. His throat felt like sandpaper. The Río Bar was empty. No sooner did he sit down than the owner, Moisés, came over. His ears were so huge everyone called him Dumbo.

"Just can't get used to seeing you in uniform, Lituma," he mocked, handing him a glass of *lúcuma* juice. You look like you're in disguise. Where are the Unstoppables?"

"They went to a cowboy movie," said Lituma, gulping down his drink. "I've got to get back to Talara right away."

"What a fucking mess that Palomino Molero business is. Did they really cut his balls off?"

"They didn't cut them off, they pulled them off." Lituma was disgusted: that was the first thing everyone wanted to know. Now Moisés would start making jokes about the kid.

"It's all the same." Dumbo moved his enormous ears as if they were the wings of some huge insect. His nose and chin also stuck way out. A total freak.

"Did you know him?"

"Yeah, and so did you, I'm sure of it. Don't you remember him? The rich boys would hire him for serenades. They had him sing at parties, at any special event, even at the Grau Club. He sang like Leo Marini, I swear. You must have met him, Lituma."

"That's what everybody says. José, Mono, and Josefino say we were all together one night when he sang at La Chunga's place. But I just can't remember it."

He closed his eyes and conjured up a series of identical nights, sitting around a small wooden table bristling with beer bottles, the cigarette smoke burning his eyes, the stink of booze, drunken voices, blurred silhouettes, and guitars playing waltzes and *tonderos*. Could he find, in that chaos,

the young, crooning, caressing voice that made you want
to dance, hold a woman, and whisper sweet nothings in her
ear? No, he couldn't turn up a thing. His cousins and
Josefino were wrong. He just drew a blank: Lituma had
never heard Palomino Molero sing in his life.

"Did you find out who killed him?"

"Not yet. Were you a friend of his?"

"He'd come by now and then to have a drink. We
weren't buddies, but we'd chat once in a while."

"Was he lively, a talker? Or was he serious and cold?"

"Quiet and shy. Romantic, kind of a poet. Too bad they
drafted him. He must have suffered with all that military
discipline."

"He wasn't drafted; he was exempt. He enlisted. His
mother can't figure it out, and neither can I."

"That's what happens when you get a broken heart."
Dumbo wagged his ears.

"That's what I think, but that doesn't tell me who killed
him or why."

Some men came into the Río Bar, and Moisés went to
take their order. It was time to find the truck driver, but
Lituma felt himself going slack. He didn't move. He saw
the slim boy tuning his guitar; he saw him in the half light
of the streets where Piura's purebreds lived, beneath the
wrought-iron bars on the balconies belonging to girls he
could never love, captivating them with his pretty voice.
He saw him pocketing the tips the rich boys would give
him for serenading their girls. Did he buy his guitar with
those tips saved up over the course of months? Why was it
a matter of "life and death" for him to leave Piura?

"Now I remember," said Moisés, flapping his ears furiously.

"What do you remember?"

"That he was crazy in love. He told me something. An impossible love. That's what he said."

"A married woman?"

"How would I know, Lituma? There's lots of impossible loves. You can fall in love with a nun, for instance. But I remember hearing him say that. 'So what are you so down in the mouth about, kid?' 'Because I'm in love, Moisés, and it's an impossible love.' That's why he joined the Air Force."

"Didn't he tell you why it was an impossible love? Or who she was?"

Moisés wagged his head and his ears.

"That's all he said. That he had to see her in secret. He serenaded her, but not under her window. From afar."

"I get it." He imagined the kid running away from Piura because of a jealous husband who'd threatened to kill him. "If we knew who the woman was, why it was an impossible love, we'd have something to go on." Maybe that's why he'd been tortured: the rage of a jealous husband.

"If it's any help to you, I can tell you that the woman he loved lived near the air base."

"Near the base?"

"One night we were talking here, Palomino Molero sitting right where you are. He heard that a friend of mine was going to Chiclayo and asked him for a ride to the air base. 'What are you going to do out there at this time of night?' 'I'm going to serenade my girlfriend, Moisés.' So she must have lived there."

"But no one lives there. It's all sand and carob trees, Moisés."

"Think about it a little, Lituma," Dumbo said, ears wagging. "Get to work on it."

"Could be." Lituma scratched his neck. "All the Air Force people and their families live right near there."

3

"RIGHT, where all the Air Force people and their families live," repeated Lieutenant Silva. "It's a real lead. Now the son of a bitch won't be able to say we're wasting his time."

But Lituma realized that even though the lieutenant was listening and talking about the meeting they were going to have with the commanding officer of the Air Force base, his body and soul were concentrated on Doña Adriana's undulations as she swept out the restaurant. Her movements occasionally raised the hem of her skirt over her knees, revealing a thick, well-turned thigh. When she bent down to pick up some garbage, her proud, unfettered breasts showed over the top of her light cotton dress. The officer's beady eyes didn't miss her slightest movement and glowed with lust.

Why was it Doña Adriana got Lieutenant Silva all hot and bothered? Lituma couldn't figure it out. The lieutenant was fair-skinned, young, good-looking, with a little blond mustache. He could have had practically any girl in Talara, but he only chased after Doña Adriana. He'd confessed as much to Lituma, "I've got that chubby broad under my skin, goddamnit." Who could figure it? She was old enough to be his mother, she had a few gray hairs in that tangle on her head, and, last but not least, she bulged all over, especially in the stomach. She was married to Matías, a fisherman who worked nights and slept during the day. They lived behind the restaurant and had several grown children who'd already moved out. Two of their boys worked for the International Petroleum Company.

"If you go on staring at Doña Adriana like that, you're going to go blind, Lieutenant. At least put on your glasses."

"You know, she gets better-looking every day," whispered the lieutenant without taking his eyes off the oscillations of Doña Adriana's broom. He rubbed his graduation ring against his trousers and added, "I don't know how she does it, but the fact of the matter is she gets better and sexier every day."

They'd had a big cup of goat's milk and sandwiches made with greasy cheese. Now they were waiting for Don Jerónimo and his taxi to take them out to the base, where Colonel Mindreau said he would see them at eight-thirty. They were the only customers in Doña Adriana's place, which was just a shanty made of bamboo poles, straw mats, and corrugated sheet metal. In one corner stood the camp stove where Doña Adriana cooked for her customers. On the other side of the back wall was the little room where Matías slept after his nights on the high seas.

"You have no idea what great things the lieutenant's been saying about you while you were sweeping, Doña Adriana," said Lituma, flashing a honeyed smile. The owner of the restaurant waddled toward him, brandishing her broom. "He says that even though you're a bit long in the tooth and a few pounds overweight you're the most tempting woman in Talara."

"I say it because I mean it." Lieutenant Silva wore his Don Juan expression. "Besides, it's true. And Doña Adriana knows it, too."

"Instead of fooling around like this with a lady who has grown children, the lieutenant ought to be out doing his job. He ought to be hunting down the murderers."

"And if I find them, what's my reward?" The lieutenant smacked his lips obscenely. "A night with you? For a reward like that I'll find them, hog-tie them, and lay them at your feet, I swear."

"He says it as if he were already slipping under the covers with her." Lituma had been enjoying the lieutenant's jokes, but then he remembered the dead kid and the jokes stopped being funny. If that damned Colonel Mindreau cooperated, things would be easier. He had to have information, files, the power to interrogate the base personnel, and if he wanted to help them, they'd find plenty of clues and then catch the sons of bitches. But Colonel Mindreau was so snooty. Why had he turned them down? Because the Air Force guys all thought they were bluebloods. They thought the Guardia Civil was a half-breed outfit they could look down on.

"Let go! Who do you think you are? Let go, or I'll wake up Matías," Doña Adriana shrieked, pulling herself free. She had handed Lieutenant Silva a pack of Incas, and he grabbed her hand. "Go feel up your maid, you fresh thing, and leave a woman with children in peace."

The lieutenant let go of her so he could light his cigarette, and Doña Adriana calmed down. It was always like that: she would get mad at his teasing and his sneaky fingers, but deep down she liked it. "There's a little whore in all of them." The thought depressed Lituma.

"That's all people are talking about in town," said Doña Adriana. "I was born here, and I've never seen anyone get killed that way before. In these parts, people kill each other fair and square, man to man. But crucifying, torturing, that's new. And you don't do anything. You should be ashamed."

"We are doing things, honey," said Lieutenant Silva. "But Colonel Mindreau isn't helping us. He won't let me question Palomino Molero's buddies. They must know something. We can't get anywhere, and it's his fault. But sooner or later the truth will come out."

"The poor mother. Colonel Mindreau thinks he's king of the hill; all you have to do is take a look at him when he comes to town with his daughter. Doesn't say hello to anyone, doesn't look at anyone. And she's even worse. What snobs!"

It wasn't even eight yet and the sun was blazing hot. The restaurant was pierced by luminous spears of light in which motes of dust floated and flies buzzed. There were few people on the street. Lituma could hear the low sound of the breaking waves and the murmur of the water washing back down the beach.

"Matías says the boy had a wonderful voice, that he was an artist," Doña Adriana said.

"Did Don Matías know Palomino Molero?" asked the lieutenant.

"He heard him sing a couple of times while he was repairing his nets."

Old Matías Querecotillo and his two assistants were loading nets and bait onto their boat, *The Lion of Talara*, when suddenly they were distracted by the strumming of a guitar.

The moonlight was so bright they didn't need a flashlight to see that the group of shadows on the beach were half a dozen airmen having a smoke there among the boats. When the boy began to sing, Matías and his boys abandoned their nets and went over to listen. The boy had a warm voice, with a vibrato that made them weepy and sent a chill up their spines. He sang "Two Souls," and when he finished they applauded. Matías Querecotillo asked permission to shake the singer's hand. "You brought the old days back to me," he congratulated him. "You've made me sad." That's when he learned that the singer's name was Palomino Molero, one of the last batch of recruits, from Piura. "You could be singing on Radio Piura, Palomino," Matías heard one of the airmen say. Since then, Doña Adriana's husband had seen him several other times, on the same beach, around the boats when they were getting *The Lion of Talara* ready to sail. Every time, they'd stopped work to listen.

"If Matías did all that, that kid must have sung like an angel, because Matías doesn't get excited that easily; he's sort of cold."

"Then he's serving you to the lieutenant on a silver platter," thought Lituma. Sure enough, the lieutenant was licking his lips like a hungry cat.

"You mean he can't cut the mustard, Doña Adrianita? I'd be happy to heat you up anytime you like. I'm like a house afire."

"I don't need anybody to heat me up." Doña Adriana laughed. "When it's cold out, I use a hot-water bottle to heat up the bed."

"Human warmth is so much nicer, honey." The lieutenant purred, puckering his lips toward Doña Adriana as if he wanted to drink her in.

Just then, Don Jerónimo appeared. He couldn't drive right up to the restaurant because the street was sandy and he'd have gotten stuck. So he'd left his Ford on the main road, about a hundred yards away. Lieutenant Silva and Lituma signed the voucher for their breakfast and bade farewell to Doña Adriana. Outside, the sun pounded them mercilessly. It was like midday even though it was eight-fifteen. In the blinding light, it seemed as if things and people might simply dissolve at any moment.

"Talara is buzzing with rumors," said Don Jerónimo as they walked toward the van, their feet sinking into the sand. "Lieutenant, you find the murderers, or they're gonna lynch you."

"Let 'em lynch me." Lieutenant Silva shrugged. "I swear I didn't kill him."

"Well, people are saying lots of strange things. Your ears must be burning."

"My ears never burn. What are they saying?"

"That you're covering up because the murderers are big shots," said Don Jerónimo, cranking up the motor. And he repeated winking at the lieutenant, "There are some big shots in this, right, Lieutenant?"

"I don't know if there are big shots or nobodies in this thing, but we'll get them no matter what. Lieutenant Silva gets his man, big or little, Don Jerónimo. So let's go, I don't want to be late for my meeting with the colonel."

The lieutenant was an honest man, and that's why Lituma esteemed and admired him. He had a big mouth, was a smooth talker, and lost his head only when it came to the plump hostess. In all the time Lituma had been working under Lieutenant Silva, he'd always seen him do his best to be fair and not play favorites.

"What have you found out up till now, Lieutenant?" Don Jerónimo blew his horn uselessly; the kids, dogs, pigs, donkeys, and goats that wandered in front of the taxi made no attempt whatever to get out of the way.

"Not a goddamn thing."

"Not much to brag about," mocked the driver.

Lituma heard his boss repeat what he'd said earlier that morning: "Today we'll find out something. You can smell it in the air."

By now they were on the outskirts of town, and on both sides of the road oil derricks punctuated the bare, rocky landscape. Off in the distance, the roofs of the Air Force base were shining in the sun. "I hope to God something turns up—anything," Lituma said to himself, echoing the lieutenant. Would they ever know who killed the kid and why? Instead of wanting justice or vengeance, he just wanted to see their faces, to hear them explain why they did what they did to Palomino Molero.

At the guardhouse, the duty officer looked them over from head to foot as if he'd never seen them before. And he kept them waiting in the white-hot sun, not thinking to ask them to sit in the shade of his office. As they waited, Lituma looked the place over:

"Shit. Talk about the good life. That's what this is." On the right were the officers' houses, all identical, all raised up on posts, all painted blue and white, with small, well-tended geranium gardens, and window screens. He saw women with children, and young girls watering flowers; he heard laughter. The airmen lived almost as well as the foreigners at the I.P.C., for chrissake! Just seeing everything so clean and neat made you jealous. They even had a pool, just behind the houses. Lituma had never seen it, but he could imagine it, full of women and kids in bathing suits, sunbathing and splashing each other.

Off to the left were the hangars and offices and, farther down, the landing strip. He could see some planes parked in a triangular formation. "They really live it up. Like the gringos at the I.P.C., these lucky bastards live like movie stars behind their fences and screens. The gringos and the Air Force people could look each other straight in the eye— right above the heads of the slobs in Talara, who were roasting down there in the town, sprawled along the dirty, oily ocean. From the base, Lituma could look right over Talara and see a rocky headland, a fence patrolled night and day by armed guards, and the houses inhabited by the engineers, technicians, and executives of the I.P.C. They, too, had their pool, complete with diving boards. In town they said the foreign women went swimming half naked.

After making them wait a long time, Colonel Mindreau finally had them sent into his office. As they walked toward the commander's door, Lituma looked at the officers and airmen. "Some of these fuckers know what happened."

Lieutenant Silva and Lituma snapped to attention at the door and then advanced to the center of the room. On the desk there was a tiny Peruvian flag, a calendar, an engagement book, some forms, a few pencils, and photographs of Colonel Mindreau with his daughter, or his daughter alone. The neatness of the office reflected the colonel's compulsive personality. Everything was in its place: the file cabinets, the diplomas on the walls, and the huge map of Peru, which served as backdrop for the commander-in-chief of the Talara Air Force Base. Colonel Mindreau was a stubby little man, barrel-chested, with a deeply lined face and a precisely trimmed salt-and-pepper mustache. The man mirrored the office. He studied them with gray, iron-cold eyes that betrayed not the slightest welcome.

"What can I do for you?" His friendly tone contradicted his glacial face.

"We're here again about the murder of Palomino Molero, sir. We need your help, Colonel," said the lieutenant.

"Haven't I already helped?" the colonel cut him off. In his low tone there was an undercurrent of mockery. "Weren't you both in this very office three days ago? If you've lost the memorandum I gave you, I have a copy."

He opened a folder he had in front of him, removed a sheet of paper, and read in a toneless voice:

"Molero Sánchez, Palomino. Born Piura, 13 February 1936. Legitimate son of Doña Asunta Sánchez and Don Teófilo Molero, deceased. Education: primary school; three years of secondary at the San Miguel National High School of Piura. Enlisted in 1953. Began tour of duty Talara Air Force Base 15 January 1954. Third Company, under command Lieutenant Adolfo Capriata. Went through basic training along with other recruits. Went AWOL on night of 23–24 March. Did not report in after a twenty-four-hour pass. Declared a deserter and reported to military police."

The colonel cleared his throat and looked at Lieutenant Silva. "Do you want another copy?"

"Why do you hate us?" thought Lituma. "And why are you such a bully, asshole?"

"No need for that, Colonel." Lieutenant Silva smiled. "We haven't lost the memorandum."

"Well, what more do you want? What kind of help can I give you? The memorandum contains everything we know about Palomino Molero. I myself carried out the investigation, in consultation with the officers, noncommissioned officers, and airmen in his company. No one saw him and no one knows who could have killed him or why. I sent my superiors a detailed report and they are satisfied. You, apparently, are not. Well, that's your problem. The staff of this base is absolutely innocent of any involvement in this matter, and there's nothing more to be learned here. Molero was a quiet fellow who didn't pal around with anyone and confided in no one. He doesn't seem to have had any friends or, for that matter, enemies on the base. According to his performance reports, he was barely mediocre. Maybe that's why he deserted. Investigate on the outside, find out who knew him in town, the people he was with from the time he deserted until he was killed. You're wasting your time here, Lieutenant, and I have no intention of wasting mine."

Lituma wondered whether the colonel's peremptory, unwavering tone would intimidate his boss and make him back down. But Lieutenant Silva stood firm.

"We didn't come here merely to waste your time, Colonel. We had a reason." The lieutenant remained at attention and spoke in a calm, measured tone.

The colonel's small gray eyes blinked once, and a menacing little smile appeared on his face. "Let's hear it then."

"Lituma here has done some investigating in Piura, Colonel."

Lituma sensed that the base commander was blushing. He felt a growing discomfort and decided he would never be able to give a convincing report to someone this hostile. Almost choking, he began to speak. In Piura he'd learned that Palomino Molero was exempt from military service but had enlisted because, as he'd told his mother, it was a matter of life and death that he get out of town. Lituma paused. Was the colonel listening? The colonel was staring at a photograph of his daughter in a setting of dunes and carob trees, his face a mixture of disgust and love.

Finally, the colonel turned toward him: "What does this 'life and death' business mean?"

"We thought he might have explained himself here, when he joined up," interjected the lieutenant. "That he might have said why he had to get out of Piura so quickly."

Was the lieutenant playing dumb? Or was he as nervous as Lituma because of the colonel's nice manners?

The base commander looked the lieutenant up and down, as if he doubted he was an officer. A stare like that should have made the lieutenant blush, but he expressed no emotion. He waited, impassively, for the colonel to say something.

"Don't you think that if we knew anything like that we would have included it in the memorandum?" The colonel spoke as if the lieutenant and Lituma were children or imbeciles. "Didn't you think that if we here on the base had known that Palomino Molero felt threatened or persecuted by someone we would instantly have informed the police or the court?"

He had to stop speaking because a nearby plane began to rev its engines. The noise finally grew so loud that Lituma thought his eardrums were going to burst. But he didn't dare clap his hands over his ears.

"Lituma found out something else, Colonel," said the lieutenant as the noise died down. He was not perturbed— as if he hadn't even heard the colonel's questions.

Mindreau turned to Lituma. "You did? What was it?"

Lituma cleared his throat to answer, but the colonel's sardonic expression silenced him. Then he blurted out: "Palomino Molero was deeply in love and it seems . . ."

"Why are you stuttering?" asked the colonel. "Not feeling well?"

"It seems it was not a proper love. That may be the reason he ran away from Piura. That is . . ."

The colonel's face had become so sour that Lituma felt stupid and he choked up. Until he walked into the commander's office, the conclusions he'd drawn the previous evening had seemed convincing to him, and the lieutenant had said, in effect, that they were valid. But now, faced with such sarcasm and skepticism, he felt unsure, even ashamed of them.

"In other words, Colonel, it may be that a jealous husband caught Palomino Molero fooling around with his wife and threatened to kill him." Lieutenant Silva came to the rescue. "And that may be why he enlisted."

The colonel looked at them silently, deep in thought. How would he insult them this time?

"Who is this jealous husband?"

"That's what we'd like to know," replied Lieutenant Silva. "If we knew that, we'd know a lot of other things."

"And do you imagine I keep up with all the affairs of the hundreds of airmen and noncommissioned officers on this base?" Colonel Mindreau returned to his sardonic school-teacher's style.

"Certainly not, Colonel," the lieutenant excused himself. "But it occurred to us that someone on the base may know something. A messmate, one of Molero's instructors, someone."

"No one knows anything about Palomino Molero's private life," the colonel interrupted again. "I myself looked into that. He was an introvert who didn't tell anyone his problems. Isn't that what it says in the memo?"

It seemed to Lituma that the colonel didn't give a shit about Palomino Molero. He hadn't shown the slightest emotion, neither this time nor the last, about the murder. He talked about the recruit as if he were a nobody, as if he weren't worth the time of day. Was it because Molero had deserted three or four days before he was killed? In addition to being nasty, the base commander was known to be a martinet, a man who went strictly by the book. Probably fed up with discipline and being locked in, the kid went AWOL, so the colonel must consider him a criminal. Deserters should be shot.

"The thing is, Colonel, we suspect that Palomino Molero was having an affair with someone on the base."

He saw that the colonel's pale, close-shaven cheeks were turning red. His expression instantly soured and he scowled. But he never got to say a word because suddenly the door opened and Lituma saw the girl in the colonel's photographs framed in the doorway, backlit by the fluorescent light in the corridor. She was very thin, more so than in the photos, with short, curly hair and a turned-up, disdainful little nose. She was wearing a white blouse, a blue skirt, tennis sneakers, and looked as bad-tempered as her father.

"I'm leaving," she said without entering the office and without acknowledging the existence of the lieutenant or Lituma. "Will the driver take me, or should I just go on my bike?"

In her way of speaking there was pent-up disgust, the same that spiced Colonel Mindreau's conversation. "A chip off the old block," thought Lituma.

"Where are you going, dear?" The commander suddenly sweetened.

"He doesn't bark at her for interrupting us, for not saying hello, or even for not speaking properly. He turns as gentle as a dove."

"*I told you this morning!* To the gringos' pool. This one's going to be crowded until Monday. Did you forget? Will the driver take me, or should I just go on my bike?"

"The driver will take you, Alicia darling. But have him come back right away; I need him. And tell him what time you want to be picked up."

The girl slammed the door and disappeared without saying goodbye. "Your daughter is our revenge," thought Lituma.

"That is . . ." the lieutenant began to say, but Colonel Mindreau cut him off: "What you've just said is pure nonsense."

"Excuse me, Colonel?"

"What proof do you have, what witnesses?" The commander-in-chief turned to Lituma and scrutinized him as if he were an insect under a magnifying glass. "Where did you get that stuff about Palomino Molero having an affair with a lady from the Piura Air Force Base?"

"I have no proof, Colonel," stammered Lituma, frightened out of his wits. "I found out that he would give serenades around here."

"At the Piura Air Force Base?" The colonel again spoke as if the lieutenant and Lituma were retarded. "Do you realize who lives there? The families of the officers. Not the families of the noncoms or airmen. Only the mothers, wives, sisters, and daughters of the officers. Are you suggesting that this airman had an adulterous affair with the wife of an officer?"

A fucking racist. That's what he was, a fucking racist.

"It might have been with one of the maids, Colonel," Lituma heard the lieutenant suggest. He thanked the lieutenant with all his heart, he felt hemmed in by the colonel's cold fury. "With a cook or a nursemaid on the base. We aren't suggesting anything, only trying to clear up this crime, Colonel. It's our job. This boy's death has turned Talara upside down. They're saying the Guardia Civil isn't doing its job because important people are involved. We're working in the dark, so we have to grab at anything that looks like a lead. Please don't take any of this personally, Colonel."

The base commander agreed, and Lituma could see the effort he was making to keep his temper in check.

"You may not know it, but until three months ago I was commander-in-chief of the Piura Air Force Base. I served there for two years. I know everything there is to know about the base, because it was my home. Nobody but nobody is going to say in front of me that a common airman is carrying on an illicit affair with the wife of one of my officers unless he can prove it."

"I never said it was an officer's wife," Lituma dared blurt out. "It could have been a maid, like the lieutenant said. There are maids on the base, aren't there? Molero would sneak over to give serenades, and that we know for a fact, Colonel."

"Okay. Find the maid, question her, question her husband about these supposed threats to Molero, and if he confesses, bring him here to me." The colonel's forehead was shining with sweat which had begun to pour out of him when his daughter burst into the office. "Don't come back here about this thing unless there's something concrete you want from me."

Abruptly he stood up, signaling that the interview was over. But Lituma noticed that Lieutenant Silva did not salute or request permission to withdraw.

"We do want something concrete from you, Colonel. We would like to question Palomino Molero's messmates."

From bright red, the base commander's face turned pale again. Purple shadows surrounded his beady eyes. "Aside from being a son of a bitch, he's loony," thought Lituma. "Why did he get like this? Where do these fits come from?"

"I'm going to explain it to you once again, Lieutenant, since it seems you haven't understood a word I've said. The Armed Forces have certain rights, they have their own courts where members of the Armed Forces are tried and sentenced. Didn't they teach you about that in the Guardia Civil Academy? No? Well, allow me to do it now. When a criminal problem involving a member of the Armed Forces arises, they themselves carry out the investigation. Palomino

Molero died under circumstances as yet unresolved, off the base, when he had been declared a deserter. I have already sent the proper report on to my superiors. If they deem it necessary, I will order a new investigation, using our own agencies. Or my superiors may decide to refer the case to the Judge Advocate's section. But until a direct order comes, either from the Air Ministry or the Commander-in-Chief of the Armed Forces, no Guardia Civil is going to violate the code of military justice in a base under my command. Is that clear, Lieutenant Silva? Answer me. Is that clear?"

"Quite clear, Colonel."

The colonel waved toward the door with a gesture that was final. "Then you may withdraw."

This time Lituma watched Lieutenant Silva click his heels and request permission to leave. He did the same and they both left. Outside, they pulled on their caps. Even though the sun beat down even harder than when they arrived and the air was even more oppressive than it had been in the office, Lituma felt refreshed and liberated out in the open air. He breathed deeply. It was like getting out of jail, goddamn it. In silence, they crossed the various squares that led back to the guard post. Did Lieutenant Silva feel as browbeaten and ill-treated as he did at the way the base commander had dealt with them?

As they left the base, they suffered yet another setback: Don Jerónimo had left them behind. The only way back to town was on foot: an hour's walk—at least—sweating bullets and swallowing dust.

They started walking down the center of the highway, still in silence. "After lunch, I'm going to take a three-hour siesta." Lituma had an unlimited capacity for sleep, at any time and in any position, and nothing cured him of the blues like a good snooze. The highway snaked around slowly, descending toward Talara through an ocher landscape devoid of green and littered with rocks and stones of all shapes and sizes. The town was a livid metallic stain below them, stretched along a motionless lead-green sea. In the intense glare they could barely make out the outlines of houses and telephone poles.

"He really put us through the ringer, didn't he, Lieutenant?" Lituma dried his brow with a handkerchief. "I've never met a guy with a worse temper. Do you think he hates the Guardia Civil just because he's a racist, or do you think he has a specific reason? Or does he treat everybody that way? Nobody, I swear, ever made me swallow so much shit as that bald bastard."

"You're out of your head, Lituma. As far as I'm concerned, the interview with Mindreau was a total success."

"Are you serious, Lieutenant? I'm glad to see you can still make jokes. As far as I'm concerned, that little chat was as depressing as it could be."

"You've got a lot to learn about this business, Lituma," said the lieutenant, laughing. "It was a bitch of an interview, let me tell you. Unbelievably useful."

"That means I didn't understand a thing, Lieutenant. It looked to me as though the colonel was treating us like scum, worse than the way he probably treats his servants. Did he even give us what we asked for?"

"Appearances are tricky, Lituma." Lieutenant Silva once again burst into laughter. "As far as I'm concerned, the colonel yakked like a drunken parrot."

He laughed again, with his mouth wide open. Then he cracked his knuckles. "Before, I thought he knew nothing, that he was fucking around with us because he wanted to protect the precious rights of the military-justice system. Now I'm sure that he knows a lot, maybe everything that happened."

Lituma looked at him again. He guessed that behind those sunglasses the lieutenant's eyes, like his face and his voice, were those of a happy man.

"You think he knows who killed Palomino Molero? Do you really think the colonel knows?"

"I don't know exactly what he knows, but he knows a lot. He's covering for someone. Why would he get so jumpy if he weren't? Didn't you see that? You're not very observant, Lituma. You really shouldn't be on the force. Those fits, that bullshit: what do you think it was all about? Pretexts to cover up his nervousness. That's the truth, Lituma. He didn't make us shit in our pants; we made him go through hell."

He laughed, happy as a lark, and he was still laughing a moment later when they heard a motor. It was a pickup truck painted Air Force blue. The driver stopped even though they hadn't flagged him down.

"Goin' to Talara?" a young warrant officer greeted them. "Hop in, we'll take you. You sit up here with me, Lieutenant; your man can sit in the back."

There were two airmen in the back of the truck who must have been mechanics because they were covered with grease. The truck was full of oil and paint in cans and paintbrushes.

"Well? You going to solve this one, or are you going to

cover things up to protect the big guys?" said one of the airmen.

There was rage in his voice.

"We'll solve it if Colonel Mindreau helps us a little," answered Lituma. "But the guy treats us like mangy dogs. Is that the way he treats all of you on the base?"

"He's not so bad. He's a straight-shooter and he makes the base work like a clock. His daughter's to blame for his bad temper."

"She really kicks him around, doesn't she?"

"She's ungrateful," said the other airman. "Colonel Mindreau has been both father and mother to her. His old lady died when the girl was still a baby. He's brought her up all by himself."

The truck stopped in front of the station. The lieutenant and Lituma jumped out.

"Lieutenant, if you don't discover who the murderers are, everyone's going to think you were bribed by the big shots," said the warrant officer, pulling away.

"Don't worry, son, we're hot on the trail." The pickup disappeared in a cloud of beer-colored dust.

4

WORD OF THE OUTRAGES being perpetrated by a certain Air Force lieutenant in the Talara whorehouse was communicated to the Guardia Civil by one of the whores. Tiger Lily had come to the station to complain that her pimp was beating her up more than usual: "He leaves me so bruised I can't turn any tricks. So I don't bring him money and he beats me up again. Explain it to him, Lieutenant Silva. I try, but it's like beating my head against a brick wall. I just can't get through."

Lilly told them that, the night before, the lieutenant had turned up at the whorehouse all alone. He tied one on, drinking *pisco* as if it were orange juice. He wasn't drinking to have a good time but to get blind drunk as quickly as possible. When he was drunk, he unzipped his fly and peed on all the whores, pimps, and customers he could reach. Then he jumped up on the bar and did a striptease until the Air Force MPs came and took him away. Liau, the Chinese who owned the place, kept everybody calm: "If somebody socks him, we all get screwed. They close me down and you're on the street. They always win, remember that."

Lieutenant Silva didn't seem to pay too much attention

to Tiger Lily's story. The next day, during lunch in Doña Adriana's place, someone else told how the pilot had repeated his act of the night before. Only this time he'd supplemented it by breaking bottles, because, as he put it, he just loved to see the little chunks of glass flying through the air. The MPs had again turned up to take him away.

By the third day, Liau himself appeared at the station, sniveling: "Last night he broke his own record. He pulled down his pants and tried to shit on the dance floor. Lieutenant, the guy's crazy. He only comes to stir up trouble, as if he wanted to get killed. Do something, because if you don't, someone's going to do him in. And I don't want that kind of trouble with the Air Force."

"Go take it up with Colonel Mindreau. It's his problem, not mine."

"I wouldn't go near Colonel Mindreau for anything in this world. I'm scared shitless of the guy. They say he goes strictly by the book."

"Well then, you're screwed, because I have no authority when it comes to the Air Force. If the guy was a civilian, I'd be only too happy to do something for you."

Liau, flabbergasted, stared at Lituma and the lieutenant. "Are you saying you can't do anything for me?"

"We'll pray for you," said the lieutenant, ushering him out. "Bye-bye, Liau. Say hello to the ladies for me."

But when Liau had gone, Lieutenant Silva turned to Lituma, who was using his best two fingers to type out the daily report on the ancient office Remington, and whispered, in a voice that sent a chill down Lituma's spine, "This business about the crazy pilot is hard to figure, don't you think, Lituma?"

"Yessir, Lieutenant." He paused a minute, then asked: "What's so hard to figure, sir?"

"Nobody throws his weight around in the whorehouse like that just for laughs. It's where all the toughest guys in Talara hang out. And three days in a row. Something smells fishy to me. Don't you think so?"

"Yessir," replied Lituma automatically, though he had no idea what Lieutenant Silva was getting at. "What do you think we ought to do?"

"We ought to go have a beer over at Liau's, Lituma. On the house, of course."

Liau's bordello had been chased from one end of Talara to the other by the parish priest. No sooner did Father Domingo catch wind of its reappearance than he demanded the mayor shut it down. A few days later, it would resurface in a shack three or four blocks away. Liau eventually won. His whorehouse was now located on the edge of town in a shed made of boards hammered together any which way. It was primitive and shaky, with a dirt floor Liau kept moist so there would be no dust and a tin roof that rattled in the wind because no one had ever bothered to nail it down. The walls of the rooms in back, where the girls worked, had so many holes that kids and drunks were always peeking in on the couples in bed.

Lieutenant Silva and Lituma slowly walked over to the bordello after seeing a cowboy movie in Mr. Frías's open-air theater—the screen was the north wall of the parish church, so Father Domingo determined which movies Frías could show.

"At least give me some idea of what you're thinking,

Lieutenant. Why do you think this crazy pilot's got anything to do with what happened to Palomino Molero?"

"I'm not thinking anything. Look, we haven't turned up a thing yet in this case, so we've got to turn over every stone to see if something's underneath. I'll take anything. We can always say that we're looking over the situation at the whorehouse and investigating the broads. Of course, the girl of my dreams won't be there."

"Now he'll start in on Fatso. What a nut."

"Last night I showed her my dick," mused Lieutenant Silva pensively. "When I went out back to piss. She was just bringing water out to her hog. She looked at me and I showed it to her. I held it like this, with both hands. 'All this is for you, baby. When will you give it what it really needs?' "

He laughed nervously, as he did whenever he talked about Doña Adriana.

"And what did she do, Lieutenant?" He knew that talking to him about Doña Adriana was the best way to tickle his fancy.

"She took off like a shot, of course. Pretended she was mad. But she saw it all right. I just know she was thinking about it. She probably dreamed about it all night. I'll bet she compared it to Don Matías's—his must be dead, all skin and no bone. I'll get to her sooner or later, Lituma. She'll go down, you'll see. And when she does, we're gonna get drunk—and we'll only drink the very best. I swear."

"Lieutenant, you're relentless. Doña Adriana ought to give in, just to reward you for all the time you've put in on her case."

There were few people in the bordello. Liau welcomed
them with open arms. "Thanks a lot for coming, Lieutenant. I knew you wouldn't let me down. Come in, come
in. Why do you think there are so few people here?
Because of that nut, what else? People come here to have
fun, not to get insulted or pissed on. Word gets around,
and nobody wants trouble with a pilot. It's not fair, right?"

"He's not here yet?"

"He usually turns up at about eleven," said Liau. "He'll
be here, just sit tight."

He seated them at a table in a dark corner and sent them
a couple of beers. A few whores came over to chat, but the
lieutenant chased them away. He couldn't pay them any
attention: he was there on men's business. Tiger Lily
thanked Lituma for threatening to throw her pimp in jail
unless he stopped beating her up, and kissed him on the
ear. "Whenever you want me, just whistle," she whispered.
"He hasn't slugged me now for three days," she added.

The pilot showed up at about midnight. Lituma and his
boss had already dispatched four beers each by then. Even
before Liau signaled them, Lituma, who had taken note of
everyone who'd come in, picked him out. Very young, thin,
dark, a crew cut. He had on the regulation khaki shirt and
trousers but wore no insignia. He came in alone, greeted no
one, was indifferent to the effect he caused—nudges, nods,
winks, and whispering among the whores and the few customers—and went directly to the bar, where he ordered a
shot. Lituma realized his heart was pounding. He didn't
take his eyes off him as the pilot tossed down the *pisco*
and ordered another.

"That's how it goes every night," whispered Tiger Lily, who was sitting at the next table with a sailor. "After the third or fourth, the show begins."

That night, the show began after the fifth or sixth. Lituma kept count, watching the lieutenant through the couples dancing to a transistor radio. The pilot rested his head on his hands and was staring fixedly at the drink he had between his elbows, as if protecting it. He didn't move. He seemed to be meditating on matters that isolated him from the whores, the pimps, and the whole world. He mechanically raised the glass to his lips. Then he became a statue again.

Between the fifth and sixth drink, Lituma looked away. When he looked back, the pilot was no longer at the bar. Lituma searched for him and found him on the dance floor. He was resolutely striding toward one of the couples: Redhead and a pudgy little fellow wearing a jacket and tie. The fat little man was dancing very carefully, holding on to the whore as if she were a life preserver. The lieutenant grabbed him by the lapel and yanked him out of the way, saying in a voice that everyone in the place could hear: " 'Scuse me, but it's my turn with the young lady."

The squat body jumped and looked around as if he wanted someone to explain just what the hell was going on and tell him what to do. Lituma saw Liau signal the guy to keep calm. Which is just what he did, shrugging his shoulders. He still looked upset, but went over to where the tarts were sitting and started to dance with Freckles. Meanwhile, the pilot was shaking around exaggeratedly, waving his hands and making faces. But there was no sign in all his clowning that he was having fun. Did he just want people to look at him? No, he wanted to be a pain in the ass, too. All that jumping and shaking gave him an excuse to elbow, shove, and bump anyone in his way. "What a motherfucker," thought Lituma. "When should they take charge?" But Lieutenant Silva went on smoking calmly, amused as he watched the pilot through puffs of smoke, as if congratulating him on his antics. The patience of those present was immense. The customers bumped by the pilot just got out of his way, smiled, and shrugged, as if to say, "What can you do with a maniac like this?" When the song was over, the pilot went back to the bar and ordered another *pisco*.

"Know who he is, Lituma?"

"No, you know him?"

"The boyfriend of Colonel Mindreau's daughter. You heard right. I saw them holding hands at the big party on Aviation Day. And Sundays, too, at Mass."

"That must be the reason the colonel puts up with all this bullshit. Anyone else he would have thrown in the brig and put on bread and water for discrediting the service."

"Talk about bullshit, watch this, Lituma."

The lieutenant had jumped up on the bar with a bottle of *pisco* in his hand and was standing there as if about to make a speech. He spread his arms wide and shouted, "Watch me empty this, assholes!" He brought the bottle to his lips and took such a big drink that Lituma's stomach began to burn as he imagined how it must feel to swallow all that hooch at once. The lieutenant's stomach must have been burning, too, because he made a face and doubled over as if he'd been punched. Liau came over, smiling, saluted, and invited him to get off the counter and stop making an uproar. But the pilot told him to fuck off and said that unless Liau kissed his ass he was going to break every bottle in the place.

Liau stepped back with a resigned expression on his face. He ran over to Lituma and Lieutenant Silva. "Aren't you going to do something?"

"Wait till he's a little drunker."

Now the pilot was daring the pimps and customers to strip, though everyone tried not to look at him and went on dancing, talking, or smoking as if he weren't there. "What'sa matter? Ashamed someone's gonna see your balls? Maybe you don't have any? Maybe they're so small you ought to be ashamed of them?" He was justifiably proud of his own balls.

"Take a good look and see what a good pair looks like!" he roared. He unbuckled his belt and Lituma saw his khaki trousers slip down, revealing skinny, hairy legs. He watched him try to kick his pants off his feet, but the more he kicked, the more entangled he became. Then he tripped and came down head first from the bar to the dance floor. The bottle in his hand smashed, his body bounced like a sack of potatoes, and the crowd started laughing.

Lieutenant Silva stood up. "Let's dance, Lituma."

Lituma followed him across the dance floor. The pilot was on his back with his eyes closed, his legs bare, his trousers twisted around his ankles, and covered with shards of glass. He was gasping. "What a fucking jolt," thought Lituma. They grabbed him under the arms and stood him up. He started swinging, muttering curses, and drooling all at the same time. They pulled up his pants, buckled his belt, and dragged him out of the bordello. The whores, pimps, and customers applauded, happy to see him go.

"Now what do we do with him, Lieutenant?"

"Let's take him over to the beach."

"Lemme go, bastards," commanded the pilot, making absolutely no attempt to get loose.

"Right away, son," said the lieutenant in a friendly way. "You just stay calm and don't get upset."

They dragged him about a hundred and fifty feet up a sandy path dotted with clumps of dry grass until they came to a sand and pebble beach. They sat him down and then sat down next to him. The neighborhood shacks were dark. The wind carried the music and noise from the bordello out to sea. It smelled of salt and fish, and the groaning tide was like a sleeping potion. Lituma felt like stretching out right there on the sand, covering his face with his cap, and forgetting the whole thing. But he'd come to work, damn it. He was nervous and worried, thinking that this semi-conscious body next to him might have some horror to reveal.

"Feeling better, buddy?" Lieutenant Silva sat the pilot up and propped him against his own body, putting his arm around his shoulders, as if they were the best of friends. "Still drunk, or are you getting over it?"

"Who the fuck are you, motherfucker?" His head was resting on the lieutenant's shoulder, and his aggressive voice was contradicted by his docile, soft body, which he was leaning against Lieutenant Silva as if against a chair back.

"I'm your friend, buddy. You should thank me for getting you out of the whorehouse. If you went on showing off your balls like that, someone might have cut them off. Do you want to end up a capon?"

He shut up because the pilot had begun to gag. He didn't vomit, but just to be on the safe side, the lieutenant turned the pilot's head away and bent him forward.

"You must be a faggot," he gasped, still furious, when he'd stopped choking. "Did you bring me here so I'd fuck you up the ass?"

"No, buddy," said Lieutenant Silva, laughing. "I brought you here so you could do me a different kind of favor."

"He's got a way of getting things out of people," thought Lituma admiringly.

"And what kind of favor do you want, motherfucker?" He hiccuped and drooled, leaning heavily on Lieutenant Silva's shoulder as if he were a kitten come to get warm next to mama.

"I want you to tell me what happened to Palomino Molero, buddy." Lituma almost jumped out of his skin.

The pilot didn't react. He neither moved nor spoke, and to Lituma it looked almost as if he'd stopped breathing. He remained frozen for quite a while. Lituma looked over at his boss. Would he repeat the question? Did the pilot understand, was he pretending he didn't?

"Maybe your mother's cunt can tell you what happened to Palomino Molero," he whimpered finally, in a voice so low that Lituma had to stretch his neck to hear. He was still nestled up against Lieutenant Silva and seemed to be trembling.

"My mama doesn't even know who Palomino Molero is, but you do. Come on, pal, tell me what happened."

"I don't know anything about Palomino Molero!" the

pilot shouted, jumping to his feet. "I don't know anything, anything at all!"

His voice had cracked and he was shaking from head to foot.

"Of course you know, pal. That's why you come to get drunk at the whorehouse every night. That's why you're half crazy. That's why you pick fights with the pimps. As if you were tired of living."

"I don't know a thing! Nothing about nothing!"

"Tell me about the kid and you'll feel better," the lieutenant went on as if petting a sick dog. "I swear you'll feel better, pal. I know, because I'm a bit of a psychologist. Let me be your confessor. I really mean it. You'll feel better."

Lituma was sweating. He felt his shirt sticking to his back, though it was actually quite cool. The breeze raised small waves that broke a few yards offshore with a nerve-racking hiss. "Lituma, what are you scared of?" he thought. "Take it easy." In his mind he could see the dead singer up there on the rocks. "Now I'm going to find out who killed him."

"Be a man and tell me. You'll feel better. And stop crying."

The pilot had begun to sob like a baby, his face buried in Lieutenant Silva's shoulder.

"I'm not crying because of what you think. I get drunk because that motherfucker knifed me in the back. He won't let me see my woman! He's ordered me not to see her. And she doesn't even want to see me, the bitch. Can you believe anyone would do that?"

"No, pal, I can't. The motherfucker who ordered you not to see your girl is Mindreau, right?"

This time, the pilot raised his head from the lieutenant's shoulder. In the moonlight, Lituma could see his face covered with snot and drool. His pupils were dilated and shiny. He moved his mouth, but no words came out.

"And why did the colonel order you to stay away from his daughter, buddy? What did you do to her? Knock her up?"

"Shh-shh! For chrissake, shut up and don't mention any names. You want to screw me up?"

"Of course I don't, pal. I'm trying to help you. I got worried seeing you like this, all fucked up, drunk, in trouble. You'll ruin your career, carrying on like this, do you realize that? Okay, I won't mention any names, I swear."

"We were going to get married as soon as my promotion went through next year. The motherfucker made me believe everything was okay, that we'd get engaged during the holidays. He screwed me, see? Did you ever hear of anyone being such a rat in your life, goddamn it?"

He'd moved, and now he was looking at Lituma.

"Never in my life," stuttered Lituma, confused.

"And who is this asshole? What's he doing here? Where'd this motherfucker come from?"

"Don't worry about him. He's okay, he's my assistant, a guy you can trust." Lieutenant Silva calmed him down again. "And don't worry about Colonel Mindreau, for that matter."

"Shh-shh. No names, damn it."

"Right, right, I forgot. Fathers are always put out when their daughters get married. They don't want to lose them. Just let time pass, he'll let up and the two of you will get married. Want some advice? Get her pregnant. Then her old man won't have any choice. Now tell me about Palomino Molero."

"Lieutenant Silva is a genius," thought Lituma.

"Her old man won't ever let up because he's not human. He's got no soul, can't you see that?" Another choking spell came over him, mixed with drunken hiccups. Lituma figured that by then his boss's shirt must have been pure slime. "A monster who's treated me like some damn nigger, get me? Now do you understand why I'm fed up? Do you understand why the only thing I can do is drink till I drop every night?"

"You better believe I understand, buddy. You're in love and you're pissed off because you can't see your woman. But who in his right mind would fall for the daughter of that bully. Come on now, pal, tell me once and for all about Palomino Molero."

"You think you're real clever, don't you?" It was as if he were no longer drunk. Lituma was about to grab him; it looked as if he might try something with Lieutenant Silva. But he didn't; he was too drunk. He couldn't sit up straight and fell over again against Lieutenant Silva.

"Come on, buddy, it'll do you good, it'll take your mind off your problem. You can forget about your girl for a minute. Did they kill him because he tried something with an officer's wife? Is that it?"

"I won't tell you a fucking thing about Palomino Molero! You can kill me first."

"That's the thanks I get for fishing you out of the whore-house alive. They would've cut your balls off. I brought you here so you could sober up and then go back to the base in good shape and not get reported. I'm your handkerchief, your pillow, and your crying towel. Just look at what you've done to my shirt, drooling all over me. And you won't even tell me why they killed Palomino Molero. Are you chicken or what?"

"He won't get a thing out of him," thought Lituma, depressed. They'd been wasting time, and, which was worse, he'd got his hopes up. This drunk wasn't going to reveal anything.

"She's a shit, too, a bigger one even than her old man," the pilot complained through clenched teeth. He choked, then gagged, then went on, "But even so I love her. Damn right. Heart and soul. And what a piece of ass."

"But why did you say your girl's a shit, too, pal? She's got to follow her old man's orders, same as you, or is it that she doesn't love you anymore? Did she tell you to get lost?"

"She doesn't know what she wants. She's her master's voice, like the little dog in the RCA ads. She only does and says what the monster tells her to. The one who told me to get lost was him speaking through her."

Lituma tried to remember exactly what the girl looked like when she made that brief appearance in her father's office. He could reconstruct the words they exchanged, but he couldn't remember if she was pretty or not. He could draw a mental picture of her silhouette—she was slim; and she must have had a strong personality, to judge by the way she talked. She was certainly vain, with a face that would have looked good on a queen. She'd wiped the floor with this poor pilot, wrecked him completely.

"Tell me about Palomino Molero, man. Anything you want. At least, if they killed him for messing around with an officer's wife over in Piura. Come on, at least that."

"I may be drunk but I'm not an asshole, and you're not gonna treat me like your nigger here." He paused and then added, bitterly, "But if you want to know something, here it is: he asked for it and he got it."

"You mean Palomino Molero?"

"Why don't you call him the motherfucker Palomino Molero."

"Right, the motherfucker Palomino Molero, if you prefer it that way," purred Lieutenant Silva, patting him on the back. "How did he ask for it?"

"Because he reached too high. Because he poached on somebody else's territory. You pay for mistakes like that. He paid, and how."

Lituma had goosebumps. This guy knew everything. He knew who killed the kid and why.

"I'm with you, buddy. A guy who reaches too high, who poaches on somebody else's territory, usually pays for it. But whose territory did he poach on?"

"Yours, motherfucker." The pilot tried to stand up. Lituma watched him crawl, get halfway up, and fall flat on his face.

"No, it wasn't my territory, pal, and you know that for a fact. It happened over in Piura, on the Air Force base. In one of the houses on the base, right?"

The pilot, still on all fours, raised his head, and Lituma thought for a second he was going to start barking. He stared at them with a glassy, anguished look, and seemed to be fighting hard against the alcohol. He was blinking incessantly.

"And who told you that, motherfucker?"

"I always remember what that Mexican comic Cantinflas says in all his movies: 'There's this little problem.' You're not the only one who knows things. I know a few things myself. I'll tell you what I know, you tell me what you know, and we'll solve this mystery together."

"First, tell me what you know about the Piura base." He was still on his hands and knees, and Lituma thought he wasn't drunk anymore. He was speaking clearly and no longer seemed afraid.

"Sure, pal. My pleasure. But sit down over here and have a smoke. You're feeling better now, right? Good."

He lit two cigarettes and handed the pack to Lituma, who took one out and lit it.

"Look, I know that Palomino Molero had a girlfriend over in the Piura base. He would serenade her with his guitar, singing in that beautiful voice he was supposed to have. Only at night and in secret. He sang her boleros, his specialty. That's it. That's all I know. Now it's your turn. Who did he serenade?"

"I don't know anything!" He was frightened again. His teeth were chattering.

"Of course you know. You know that the husband of the woman he serenaded found out about it, or maybe caught them in the act. And you know that Molero had to get out of Piura on the double. That's why he came here and enlisted in Talara. But the jealous husband found out where he was, came looking for him, and bumped him off. For doing just what you said, pal. For reaching too high, for poaching on someone else's territory. Come on, don't hold back. Who did it?"

The pilot started gagging again. This time he vomited, bent over, and made spectacular noises. When he'd finished, he wiped his mouth with his hand and began to grimace. He ended up crying like a baby. Lituma was disgusted and sorry for him. The poor guy was really suffering.

"You wonder why I keep asking you to tell me who it was." The lieutenant was blowing smoke rings. "Curiosity, pal, that's all. If the guy who killed the kid was from the Piura base, what can I do? Nothing. You all have your own laws and rights, your own courts. I can't even stick my nose in. Just curiosity, see? And besides, I want to tell you something. If I were married to a certain chubby woman I know, and someone came to serenade her and sing her romantic boleros, I'd nail him, too. Who knocked off Palomino Molero, pal?"

Even at a time like that, he was thinking about Doña Adriana. He was sick. The pilot moved away from his own vomit and sat down on the sand, in front of Lituma and his boss. He put his elbows on his knees and buried his face in his hands. He must be feeling the tail end of the booze. Lituma could remember that feeling of emptiness and chills, an undefined, general malaise he knew only too well from his days as an Unstoppable.

"And how did you find out he serenaded her on the Piura base?" At times he seemed frightened, at others mad, and now he was both at once. "Who the fuck told you?"

Just then, Lituma noticed shadows moving toward them. A few seconds later, they were standing in a half circle right in front of them. There were six. They carried rifles and billyclubs, and in the moonlight Lituma recognized their armbands. Air Force MPs. They patrolled the bars, parties, and the bordello, picking up any Air Force personnel making trouble.

"I'm Lieutenant Silva of the Guardia Civil. Something wrong?"

"We've come to pick up Lieutenant Dufó."

"Brush your teeth before you say my name, boy." He managed to get up on his feet, although he weaved back and forth as if he might lose his balance at any moment. "No one takes me anywhere, goddamn it."

"Colonel's orders, Lieutenant. Sorry, but we have to take you back."

The pilot rasped out something and slowly collapsed on the ground. The warrant officer gave an order and the other silhouettes closed in. They picked up Lieutenant Dufó by his arms and legs and carried him off. He let them, mumbling some incomprehensible complaint.

Lituma and Lieutenant Silva watched them disappear in the darkness. In a few minutes, they heard a far-off jeep start up. They finished their cigarettes in silence, absorbed in thought. The lieutenant got up first to begin the trip back. As they passed the whorehouse, they heard music, voices, and laughter. A full house.

"You really are something for getting people to spill their guts, Lieutenant. What a job you did, bringing him along until he told at least something."

"I didn't get all he knows. If we'd had more time, he might have told the whole story." He spit and took a deep breath, as if to fill his lungs with the sea air. "I'll tell you something, Lituma. Know what I think?"

"What, Lieutenant?"

"That on the base everybody knows what happened. From the cook to Mindreau."

"I wouldn't be surprised. At least that's the impression I got from Lieutenant Dufó. That he knows perfectly well who killed Molero."

They walked a good distance in silence through a sleeping Talara. Most of the wooden shacks were dark, except for an occasional candle. Up above, behind the fences in the restricted zone, it was also pitch-dark.

Suddenly the lieutenant spoke in a different tone of voice. "Lituma, how'd you like to do me a big favor? Go down to the fishermen's wharf and see if *The Lion of Talara* has set sail. If it's gone, just go to bed. But if it's still there, I'll be over at Doña Adriana's."

"What, Lieutenant? This must mean that . . ."

"It means I'm going to make my move. I don't know if tonight's the night. Maybe yes, maybe no. But why not take a shot at it? It's taking much longer than I ever thought it would, but someday it's gonna happen. Know why? Because I've made a vow: I won't die until I screw that fat bitch and until I find out who killed Palomino Molero. Those are my two goals in life, Lituma. Even more important than a promotion—although I wouldn't take that too seriously if I were you. Go on, get going."

"How can he feel like doing that now?" He thought about Doña Adriana curled up in her bed, dreaming, unaware of the visit she was going to get. "Damn! What a crazy fucker this Lieutenant Silva'd turned out to be. Would he screw her tonight? No way." Lituma was sure

Doña Adriana would never give in. Most of the boats had already sailed, and there were only a half dozen on the beach. *The Lion of Talara* was not one of them. He checked them one by one to be sure. Just as he was leaving, he noticed a shadow leaning against one of the beached boats.

"Good evening."

"Evening," said the woman, as if annoyed at being interrupted.

"For God's sake, what are you doing here at this hour of the night, Doña Adriana?" She wore a black shirt over her dress and was barefoot, as usual.

"I came to bring Matías his lunch. And after he left, I stayed to cool off. I'm not sleepy. And you, Lituma? What brings you down here? Meeting a girl?"

Lituma laughed. He hunkered down in front of Doña Adriana, taking advantage of the dim light to examine her abundant figure, those generous curves Lieutenant Silva lusted after.

"What are you laughing at? Have you gone crazy, or are you drunk? I know, you've been over at Liau's place."

"Nothing like that, Doña Adriana. If I tell you, you'll die laughing, too."

"Tell me, then. And don't laugh by yourself like that; you look like a jerk."

Doña Adriana was usually in a good mood and was a spirited woman, but Lituma could see that tonight she was a bit melancholy. She had her arms crossed in front of her chest and was digging in the sand with one foot.

"Something bothering you, Doña Adriana?" Now Lituma was serious.

"Bothering me? No. But something's got me worried, Lituma. Matías won't go to the clinic. He's so stubborn, and I can't convince him."

She paused and sighed. She said that for at least a month her husband had been hoarse and when he coughed hard he brought up blood. She bought him some medicine at the pharmacy and almost had to force it down his throat, but it hadn't helped. It might be something serious you couldn't cure with drugstore medicine. He might need X-rays or an operation. He wouldn't even hear of going to the clinic; he always said it would go away by itself, that only fairies went to the doctor for a cough. But he couldn't fool her: he felt worse than he let on, because every night it got harder for him to go out fishing. He forbade her to mention the spit-up blood to their sons. But she was going to tell them anyway on Sunday when they usually visited. Maybe they could drag him to a doctor.

"You really love Don Matías, don't you, Doña Adriana?"

"We've been together for almost twenty-five years. It seems incredible how fast the years go by. Matías caught me when I was just a girl, about fifteen years old. I was afraid of him because he was so much older. But he kept after me for so long that he finally wore down my resistance. My folks didn't want me to marry him. People said he was so much older that the marriage couldn't last. But they were wrong, see? It's lasted, and through it all we've gotten along pretty well together. Why did you ask me if I love him?"

"Because now I'm a little ashamed to tell you what I was doing here."

The foot digging in the sand stiffened a few inches away from where Lituma was hunched down.

"Stop being mysterious, Lituma. Or is this a guessing game?"

"Lieutenant Silva sent me down to see if Don Matías has gone out to sea," he whispered in a malicious tone. He waited, and since she asked no more questions, he added: "Because he went to pay you a visit, Doña Adriana, and he didn't want your husband to catch him. He must be knocking on your door right now."

There was a silence. Lituma heard the nearby waves lapping on the shore. After a moment, he heard her laughing, slowly and mockingly, holding it in, as if she didn't want him to hear. He started to laugh all over again. And they both laughed out loud.

"It's not right for us to be laughing at the lieutenant's passion this way, Doña Adriana."

"He must still be there, knocking at the door and scratching at the window, begging and begging for me to let him in. Promising me the moon and the stars if I let him in. Ha-ha-ha! Talking to the man in the moon! Ha-ha-ha!"

They laughed some more, and when they fell silent, Lituma saw that Doña Adriana's foot had again begun to dig methodically and obstinately in the sand. In the distance, the refinery whistle blew, announcing a new shift. He could also hear the sounds of trucks out on the highway.

"The truth is, the lieutenant's crazy about you. If you ever heard him. He doesn't talk about anything else. He doesn't even look at other women. For him, you're the Queen of Talara."

He heard Doña Adriana give a pleased little laugh. "He's got a dozen hands, that guy, and someday he'll get slapped for getting fresh with me. Crazy about me? It's just a game, Lituma. He's got it in his head that he's got to conquer me, and since I won't give in, he won't give up. Do you think I can believe that a boy like him is in love with a woman who's old enough to be his mother? I'm not a fool, Lituma. Some fun, that's all he wants. If I did it just once, you'd never hear another word about love."

"And are you going to do it—just once—Doña Adriana?"

"Not a chance in the world." Her voice was angry, but Lituma could see she was faking. "I'm not one of those women. I have a family, Lituma. No man but my husband touches me."

"Well, the lieutenant's going to die then, Doña Adriana. Because I swear I've never seen a man as much in love with anyone as he's in love with you. He even talks to you in his sleep, imagine that."

"And what does he say to me in his sleep?"

"I can't tell you that; it's dirty."

When she finished giggling, she stood up with her arms still crossed and walked off. She went toward the restaurant followed by Lituma.

"I'm glad we ran into each other. You made me laugh and forget my worries."

"I'm happy, too, Doña Adriana. Our talk made me forget the dead kid. He's been on my mind ever since I saw him up in the pasture. Sometimes I even get nightmares. I hope tonight I won't."

He said goodbye to Doña Adriana at the door of her restaurant and walked to the station. He and the lieutenant slept there, Silva in a large room next to the office and Lituma in a sort of shed near the cells. As he walked through the deserted streets, he imagined the lieutenant scratching at the restaurant windows and whispering words of love to the empty air.

At the station, he found a piece of paper stuck on the door handle so someone would see it. He carefully took it down, went inside, and turned on the light. The note had been written in blue ink by an educated person with good handwriting:

> *Palomino Molero's killers kidnapped him*
> *from Doña Lupe's house in Amotape. She*
> *knows what happened. Ask her.*

The station regularly received anonymous notes, usually about unfaithful wives or husbands or about smugglers. This was the first about the death of Palomino Molero.

5

"AMOTAPE, what kind of a name is that?" asked Lieutenant Silva sarcastically. "Can it be true that it comes from that story about the priest and his maid? What do you think, Doña Lupe?"

Amotape is thirty miles south of Talara, surrounded by sun-parched rocks and scorching sand dunes. There are dry bushes, carob thickets, and here and there a eucalyptus tree—pale green patches that brighten the otherwise monotonous gray of the arid landscape. The trees bend over, stretch out and twist around to absorb whatever moisture might be in the air; in the distance they look like dancing witches. In their benevolent shade, herds of squalid goats are always nibbling the crunchy pods that fall off their branches; there are also some sleepy mules and a shepherd, usually a small boy or girl, sunburnt, with bright eyes.

"Do you think that old story about Amotape with the priest and his maid is the truth, Doña Lupe?"

The hamlet is a confusion of adobe huts and little corrals made from wooden stakes. It has a few aristocratic houses clustered around an old plaza with a wooden gazebo. There are almond trees, bougainvilleas, and a stone monument to Simón Rodríguez, Simón Bolívar's teacher, who died in this solitary place. The citizens of Amotape, poor, dusty folks, live off their goats, their cotton fields, and the truck and bus drivers who detour between Talara and Sullana in order to drink some *chicha*, the local corn beer, or have a snack.

The name of the town, according to local legend, comes from colonial times, when Amotape, a rich town then, had a greedy parish priest who hated to feed visitors. His maid abetted him in this by warning him whenever she saw a traveler approaching. She would call out, "Amo, tape, tape la olla, que viene gente" (Master, cover, cover the pot, people are coming). Could it be true?

"Who knows," murmured the woman at last. "Maybe yes, maybe no. God only knows."

She was very thin with olive-colored parchment-like skin that sagged and hung from her cheekbones and upper arms. From the moment she saw them coming, she had a look of distrust on her face. "More distrust than people usually have on their faces when they spot us," thought Lituma. She studied them with deep-sunk, frightened eyes, and occasionally rubbed her arms as if she'd felt a chill. When her eyes met theirs, she tried to smile, but it was so false it made her look like a cheap whore. "You're scared shitless, lady," thought Lituma. "You know something." She'd looked at them like that as she served them fried and salted banana chips and stewed kid with rice. And she went on looking at them like that every time the lieutenant asked her to refill their gourds with *chicha*.

When would Lieutenant Silva start asking her questions? Lituma felt the corn beer going to his head. It was high noon and hot as hell. He and the lieutenant were the only customers. Looking out the door, they could see the slumped-over little Church of St. Nicholas, heroically resisting the passage of time. A few hundred yards beyond the dunes was the highway and the trucks going to Sullana or Talara. Lituma and the lieutenant had hitched a ride on a truck loaded with chickens. They'd been dropped off on the highway, and as they walked through the town, they'd seen curious faces pop out of every shack in Amotape. The lieutenant asked which place was Doña Lupe's, and the chorus of kids around them instantly pointed out the place where he and Lituma were now sipping *chicha* out of gourds.

Lituma sighed in relief. At least the woman existed, so the trip might not be a wild-goose chase. They'd had to ride on the back of the truck, deafened by the clucking, with the smell of chicken shit in their noses and with feathers flying in their mouths and ears. The unrelenting sun had given them a headache. When they went back to Talara, they'd have to walk all the way to the highway, stand there, and wait until some truck driver condescended to give them a lift.

"Afternoon, Doña Lupe," Lieutenant Silva had said as they walked in. "We've come to see if your *chicha*, your banana chips, and your kid stew are as good as people say. We've heard a lot of good things about your place; I hope you don't let us down."

Judging by the way she looked at them, Doña Lupe hadn't swallowed the lieutenant's story. Especially, thought Lituma, when you consider how sour her *chicha* is and how tasteless this stew is. At first there were children crowding around them, but little by little they got bored and drifted out. Now the only ones left in the shack were three half-naked little girls sitting around the stove playing with some empty gourds. They must have been Doña Lupe's daughters, though it was hard to see how a woman her age could have such young kids. Maybe she wasn't as old as she looked. All their attempts to strike up a conversation with her failed. They'd talked about the weather, the drought, this year's cotton crop, how Amotape got its name—and she'd answered every question the same way: yes, no, I don't know, or just plain silence.

"I'm going to say something that's going to surprise you, Lituma. You think Doña Adriana's fat, right? Well, you're wrong. What she is is plump, which is not the same as being fat."

When was the lieutenant going to get started? How would he do it? Lituma couldn't sit still; his boss's tricks constantly surprised him and aroused his admiration. It was clear that Lieutenant Silva was as eager as he was to untangle the mystery surrounding Palomino Molero's death, and he'd seen how excited the lieutenant had become when he read the anonymous letter. Sniffing at the paper like a bloodhound sniffing a trail, he declared, "This isn't bullshit. It's a promising lead. We've got to go to Amotape."

"Know the difference between a fat woman and a plump woman, Lituma? A fat woman is soft, covered with rolls, spongy. You poke her, and your hand sinks in as if she were made of cottage cheese. You think you've been fooled. A plump woman is hard, filled-out, she's got what it takes and more. Everything in the right places. It's all well distributed and well proportioned. You poke her and your

finger bounces off. There's always enough, more than
enough, enough to take all you want and even to give some
away."

All the way to Amotape, as the desert sun bore its way
through their caps, the lieutenant kept on talking about
the anonymous note, speculating about Lieutenant Dufó,
Colonel Mindreau, and his daughter. But from the moment
they entered Doña Lupe's shack, it was as if his interest in
Palomino Molero had gone into eclipse. As they ate, he
talked only about how Amotape got its name, or—of course
—about Doña Adriana. And out loud to boot, totally un-
concerned that Doña Lupe might hear his lascivious
remarks.

"It's the difference between fat and muscle, Lituma. A
fat woman is pure lard. A plump woman is pure muscle.
Tits that are pure muscle—that's the best thing in the
world! Even better than this stewed kid of Doña Lupe's.
Don't laugh, Lituma, it's the God's honest truth. You don't
know about these things, but I do. A big, muscular ass,
muscular thighs, shoulders, hips: isn't that a lovely dish to
set before a king? God almighty! That's the way my baby
back in Talara is, Lituma. Not fat, but plump. A woman
who's pure muscle, goddamn it. Just what I like."

Lituma laughed because it was his duty to laugh, but
Doña Lupe remained serious throughout the lieutenant's
discourse, scrutinizing the two of them. "She's waiting,"
thought Lituma, "probably as nervous as I am." When
would the lieutenant get going? He acted as if he had all
the time in the world. And he just never gave up talking
about the fat love of his life.

"You might well be wondering how it is that I know Doña Adrianita is plump and not fat. Does that mean I've touched her? Just here and there, Lituma, just here and there. Quick feels. It's dumb, I know it. And you're right to think it. But the fact is that I've seen her. There it is, now I've told you my biggest secret. I've seen her bathing in her slip over on that little beach behind Crab Point where all the Talara women go so the men won't see them. Why do you think I disappear all the time at about five in the afternoon with my binoculars? I tell you I'm going to have coffee over at the Hotel Royal. Why do you think I climb up that point by that little beach? What else, Lituma? I go to see my honey bathing in her pink slip. When that slip gets wet, it's as if she had nothing on at all, Lituma. God almighty! Get out the fire extinguisher, Doña Lupe, I'm on fire! Put out this blaze! Now that's where you can see a plump body, Lituma. That hard ass, those hard tits, pure muscle from head to toe. Someday I'll take you with me and show you. I'll lend you my binoculars. Then you'll really get cross-eyed. And you'll see how right I am. That's right, Lituma, I'm not jealous, at least of enlisted men. If you behave yourself, I'll take you out to the point. You'll be in heaven when you see that Amazon."

It was as if he'd forgotten why they'd come to Amotape, goddamn it. But just when Lituma's impatience had reached its limit, Lieutenant Silva suddenly fell silent. He took off his sunglasses—Lituma saw that his eyes were bright and incisive—cleaned them with his handkerchief, and put them on again.

He calmly lit a cigarette and began to speak in honeyed

tones: "Excuse me, Doña Lupe. Come on over here a minute and sit down with us, will you? We have to have a little talk, okay?"

"What about?" Her teeth were chattering, and she was shaking so much it was as if she had malaria. Lituma realized that he, too, was trembling.

"About Palomino Molero, Doña Lupe, what else could it be? I wouldn't talk with you about my sweetie over in Talara, my little chubby, right? Come on, sit right here."

"I don't know who you're talking about." She sat down like a robot on the bench the lieutenant had pointed to. She seemed to have shriveled and gotten thinner than before. "I swear I don't know who that is."

"Of course you know who Palomino Molero is, Doña Lupe." The lieutenant was no longer smiling and spoke in a cold, hard tone that caught even Lituma off-guard: "Okay, now we're going to find out what happened." Lieutenant Silva went on: "You remember him, Doña Lupe. The Air Force guy they killed over in Talara. The one they burned with cigarettes and then hung. The one who got a stick shoved up his backside. Palomino Molero, a skinny kid who sang boleros. He was here, right where we are now. Now do you remember?"

Lituma saw the woman open her eyes and her mouth, but she said nothing. She stood there like that, her eyes jumping out of her head. One of the little girls started to cry.

"I'll be honest with you." The lieutenant exhaled a mouthful of smoke and seemed distracted, watching the smoke disappear. Suddenly he went on, in a harsh voice: "If you don't cooperate, if you don't answer my questions, there's going to be a fucking mess here the likes of which you've never seen. I'll tell you right out, bad words and all, so you can see how serious it is. I don't want to have to take you in, to bring you all the way to Talara and throw you in jail. I don't want you to spend the rest of your life in jail for having withheld evidence and being an accomplice after the fact. I assure you that I don't want any of that, Doña Lupe."

The child continued to whimper, and Lituma put his finger on his lips to tell her to keep still. She stuck out her tongue and smiled.

"They'll kill me." She moaned, but she wasn't crying. There was animal fear in her dry eyes. Lituma didn't dare take a breath, because he imagined that if he moved or made a sound something bad would happen.

He saw that Lieutenant Silva very carefully undid his holster, took out his service revolver, and put it on the table, shoving the remains of the goat stew to one side. He patted the pistol as he spoke: "No one's going to lay a hand on you, Doña Lupe. As long as you tell us the truth. I'll defend you myself if it comes to that."

The crazy braying of a donkey broke the silence of the world outside the shack. "They're breeding her," thought Lituma.

"They threatened me. They said, 'If you talk, you're dead,' " howled the woman, raising her arms over her head. She squeezed her face between her hands and twisted her entire body. Her teeth were chattering loudly. "It's not my fault, what did I do, sir? I can't die and leave my babies alone in the world. My husband was killed by a tractor, sir."

The children playing in the dirt turned when they heard

her scream, but after a few seconds they lost interest and went back to their games. The one who'd started to cry had crawled to the doorway of the cabin.

"They took out their guns too, so who should I believe, them or you?" She tried to cry, made faces, rubbed her arms, but her eyes were still dry. She beat her breast and made the sign of the cross.

Lituma took a look outside. No, her screams had not brought out the neighbors. Through the doorway and even through some of the cracks in the walls, you could see the closed door of St. Nicholas Church as well as the deserted plaza. The children, who up to a minute ago had been kicking a rag ball around the wooden gazebo, were no longer there. "They've called them and hidden them. Their parents grabbed them by the neck and dragged them into the shacks so they wouldn't see or hear what was going to happen here." They all knew about Palomino Molero. They were all witnesses. Now for sure the mystery would be solved.

"Calm down, let's go over this thing one piece at a time. We're in no hurry." But again the lieutenant's tone contradicted his words: he didn't want to calm her down but get her even more frightened. He was cold and threatening: "Nobody's going to touch you. I swear on my honor. Providing you tell the truth. Providing you tell me everything you know."

"I don't know anything, nothing. I'm afraid, my God." But anyone could see in her face, in her dejection, that she knew everything and that she had no strength left to deny it. "Help me, St. Nicholas."

She crossed herself twice and kissed her crossed fingers.

"Start at the beginning. When and why did Palomino Molero come here? How long did you know him?"

"I didn't know him. I'd never seen him before in my life." Her voice rose and fell, as if she'd lost control of her throat. Her eyes were rolling in her head. "I wouldn't have let him stay here if it hadn't been for the girl. They were looking for the priest, Father Ezequiel. But he wasn't here, almost never is, traveling around the way he does."

"The girl?" Lituma blurted out. A glance from the lieutenant made him bite his tongue.

"The girl. She was the one. They begged me so much that I felt sorry for them. I didn't even get any money out of it, sir, and God knows I need it. My husband was run over by a tractor, I told you, didn't I? I swear by God in heaven and by St. Nicholas, our patron saint. The two of them didn't have a cent. Just enough to pay for their dinner, that's it. I gave them the bed for nothing. Because they were going to get married. I was sorry for them, they were so young, just kids, and they seemed so much in love, sir. How could I know what was going to happen? Oh, God, what did I do that you should give me such heartache?"

The lieutenant, blowing smoke rings and glaring at the woman through his sunglasses, waited for her to cross herself, squeeze her arms, and rub her face as if trying to erase it.

"I know you're honest. I could see that the moment I walked through the door. Don't worry about anything, just go on talking. How many days were the lovebirds here?"

Again the obscene braying pierced the morning air. Nearer this time. And Lituma also heard galloping hooves. "That's done her," he deduced.

"Only two days. They were waiting for the priest, Father Ezequiel, but he was away. He always is. He says he goes to baptize children and marry people out on the haciendas in the mountains, that he goes to Ayabaca because he's so devoted to the statue of Our Lord in Captivity there, but who knows. People say a thousand different things about all that traveling around. I told them not to wait, because Father Ezequiel might not be back for a week or ten days, who could tell. They were leaving the next day for San Jacinto. It was Sunday and I myself advised them to go there. On Sundays, a priest from Sullana goes to San Jacinto to say Mass. He could marry them in the hacienda chapel. That's what they wanted most in the world, a priest to marry them. Here they were wasting their time waiting around. Go to San Jacinto, that's what I told them."

"But the lovebirds didn't get to San Jacinto that Sunday."

"No." Doña Lupe was struck dumb and looked back and forth from Lituma to the lieutenant. She trembled and her teeth chattered.

"They didn't get to San Jacinto that Sunday because . . ." Lieutenant Silva helped her along.

"Because someone came looking for them on Saturday afternoon," the terrified woman whispered, her eyes jumping out of her head.

It still wasn't dark. The sun was a ball of fire among the eucalyptus and carob trees; the tin roofs of some houses reflected the blazing sunset. She was bent over the stove cooking and stopped when she saw the car. It left the highway, turned toward Amotape, bounced, raised a dust cloud, and ground its way straight to the plaza. Doña Lupe watched every inch of the way as it approached. They, too, heard and saw it. But they paid it no attention until it skidded to a halt in front of the church. They were sitting there kissing. They were kissing all the time. Stop it, now, you're setting a bad example for the children. Why don't you talk or sing.

"Because he sang beautifully, didn't he?" whispered the lieutenant, encouraging her to go on. "Mostly boleros, right?"

"Waltzes and *tonderos*, too." She sighed so loud that Lituma jumped. "And even *cumananas*, you know, what they sing when two singers challenge each other. He did it really well, he was so funny."

"The car rolled into Amotape and you saw it," the lieutenant reminded her. "Did they run away? Did they hide?"

"She wanted him to run away and hide. She scared him, saying, Run away, honey, go away, run, run, don't stay here, I don't want them to . . ." "No, sweetheart, remember, you're mine now. We've spent two nights together, you're my wife. Now nobody can come between us. They'll have to accept our love. I'm not leaving. I'll wait for him, talk to him."

"She was scared out of her wits, run, run, if they catch you, they'll . . . I don't know what, get out of here, I'll keep them here, I don't want them to kill you, darling." She was so scared that Doña Lupe also got scared: "Who are they?" she asked the young couple, pointing at the dusty car, the silhouettes that got out and stood anonymously framed by the burning horizon. "Who's coming? My God! What's going to happen?"

"Who was coming, Doña Lupe?" asked the lieutenant, blowing smoke rings.

"Who do you think it was? Who else could it be but your kind?"

Lieutenant Silva didn't move a muscle. "You mean the Guardia Civil? Or do you mean the military police from the Talara Air Force Base? Is that it?"

"Your kind. Men in uniforms. Isn't it all the same thing?"

"Actually it isn't. But it doesn't matter."

At that moment, even though he missed not a one of Doña Lupe's revelations, Lituma saw them. They were sitting right there, in the shade, holding hands, an instant before disaster struck. He'd bent his head covered with short, black curls over her shoulder and, caressing her ear with his lips, was singing to her: "Two souls joined by God in this world, two souls who loved each other, that's what we were, you and I." Moved by the tenderness and the beauty of his voice, she had tears in her eyes, and so she could hear him better, she shrugged her shoulders and crinkled up her loving face. There was no evidence of nastiness or arrogance in those adolescent features sweetened by love.

Lituma felt desolated by sadness as he imagined the vehicle of the uniformed men: first a roaring motor, then clouds of yellow dust. It traced a path around midday Amotape and after a few horrid moments stopped a few yards from the very doorless shack where they were now. "At least he must have been very happy during the two days he spent here."

"Only two men?" Lituma was surprised to see the lieutenant so surprised. He avoided looking him in the eye, out of an obscure superstition.

"Only two," repeated the woman, nervous and uncertain. She squinted toward the ceiling, as if trying to figure out where she'd made her mistake. "Nobody else. They got out and the jeep was empty. Yes, a jeep. There were only two of them, I'm sure. Why do you ask, sir?"

"No reason," said the lieutenant, grinding his cigarette butt on the floor with his shoe. "I would have thought that at least a patrol would have come for them. But if you saw two, there were two and that's that. Go on."

Another bray interrupted Doña Lupe. It floated in the scorching midday atmosphere of Amotape, prolonged, full of high and low notes, deep, funny, seminal. As soon as they heard it, the children playing on the floor got up and ran or toddled out, splitting their sides with malicious laughter. "They're going to find the mare and see how the donkey mounts her and makes her yell like that," Lituma thought.

"Are you all right?" said the shadow of the older man, the shadow that did not have a pistol in its hand. "Did he hurt you? Are you all right?"

It had suddenly gotten dark. In the few seconds it had taken for the two men to walk the short distance from the jeep to the shack, the afternoon had turned to night.

"If you hurt him, I'll kill myself," said the girl, not shouting but challenging, her heels firmly planted on the ground, her fists tight, her chin shaking. "If you touch him, I'll kill myself. But before I do, I'll tell everything. Everyone will be ashamed and disgusted at you."

Doña Lupe was shaking like a leaf. "What's going on,

sir? Who are you? What can I do for you? This is my own little place, I mind my own business. I'm just a poor woman."

The shadow with the weapon, who flashed fire whenever he looked at the boy—the older one looked only at the girl —went up to Doña Lupe and put his pistol between her withered breasts. "We're not here, we don't even exist," he instructed her, drunk with hate and fury. "Open your mouth and you're a dead bitch. I'll blow your brains out. Understand?"

She went down on her knees, begging. She knew nothing, understood nothing. "What did I do, sir? Nothing, nothing. I took in two kids who asked for a room. For the love of God, think of your own mother, sir, don't shoot, we don't want any trouble or disgrace around here."

"Did the younger man call the older one *colonel*?"

"I don't know, sir," she replied, trying to find her way through the interrogation. She was trying to guess what he wanted her to say. "*Colonel*? The younger addressing the older one? Maybe he did, maybe he didn't. I don't remember. I'm a poor, ignorant woman, sir. I don't have anything to do with all this, it was all an accident. The one with the gun said that if I opened my mouth and told what I'm telling you, he'd come back and blow my brains out, then shoot me in the stomach, and then shoot me between the legs. What could I do, what was I going to do? I lost my husband, he was run over by a tractor. I've got six kids and I can just barely feed them. I had thirteen, and seven died. If I get killed, the other six will die. Is that fair?"

"The one with the gun, was he an officer? Did he have stripes on his shoulder or just a silver bar on his cap?"

Lituma began to believe in telepathy. His boss was asking the very questions he was thinking. He was panting, feeling dizzy.

"I don't know what you're talking about. Can't you stop torturing me? Don't ask me questions I don't understand. What are stripes? What are you talking about?"

Lituma heard her, but he was seeing the young couple again, clearly, despite the blue shadows that covered Amotape. Doña Lupe, on her knees in front of the frenetic, gesticulating young man, was whimpering right there on the doorstep; the old man's staring eyes were bitterly, painfully, disdainfully on the girl, who defiantly protected the thin boy with her own body and kept him from stepping up to the men in uniform. Lituma was seeing how the arrival of the outsiders had taken the children, the old people, and even the dogs and goats of Amotape off the streets and buried them in their houses. Everyone was afraid of getting involved in this kind of trouble.

"You keep quiet, keep your mouth shut, who do you think you are, who gave you the right, what are you doing here anyway," said the girl, protecting him, pushing him out, holding him back, stopping him from speaking. At the same time she kept on threatening the shadow of the older man: "I'll kill myself and tell the world everything."

"I love her with all my heart, I'm an honorable man, I'll dedicate my life to loving her and making her happy." No matter how he tried, the boy couldn't get around the body of the girl who was shielding him, in order to come forward. The old man's shadow never turned toward him but remained fixed on the girl, as if no one else existed in Amotape or the world for that matter. But the young man half turned the instant he heard the boy speak and lunged toward him, muttering curses and waving his pistol as if he were going to smash in the boy's head. The girl grabbed him and tangled him up. Then the shadow of the older man gave a dry, definitive order: "At ease," which the other obeyed instantly.

"All he said was *At ease*? Or did he say *At ease, Dufó*? or maybe *At ease, Lieutenant Dufó*?"

This went beyond telepathy. The lieutenant asked the questions using the same words that came to Lituma. "I don't know," swore Doña Lupe. "I never heard any names. I only found out that his name was Palomino Molero when I saw the photos in the Piura newspaper. I recognized him right away. My heart broke, sir. That's him, the kid who ran away with the girl and brought her to Amotape. But I never found out her name or the names of the men who came looking for them. And I don't want to know, either. Don't tell me if you know. I'm cooperating, okay? Don't mention their names!"

"Don't get upset, stop shouting, don't say those things," said the shadow of the old one. "Child, how can you think of threatening me? You're going to kill yourself, you?"

"If you hurt him, if you touch a hair on his head." In the sky, behind a bluish haze, the shadows grew darker. The stars had come out. Some candles began to flicker among the adobe walls, cast-iron gates, and bamboo fences of Amotape.

"Hurt him? I'm going to shake hands with him and say to him, from the bottom of my heart, 'I forgive you,'" murmured the shadow of the old one. He actually did extend his arm toward him, although he was yet to look at him. Doña Lupe began to feel better. She saw they were shaking hands. The boy was so overcome with emotion he could barely speak.

"I swear to you, I'll do anything, she's the light of my life, the holiest thing, she . . ."

"Now you two have to shake hands as well," ordered the older shadow. "No grudges. No rank here. Just two men, three men, arranging their affairs, the way real men always do things. Happy now, dear? Calmed down? That's right, it's all over now. Let's get out of here."

He quickly took his wallet out of his back pocket. Doña Lupe felt the sweat-moistened bank notes in her hand and heard a gentlemanly voice thanking her for all her trouble and advising her to forget the whole thing. Then she saw the shadow of the older man walk out of the shack toward the jeep. But the younger shadow poked its pistol in her chest again before leaving: "If you open your mouth, you know what will happen to you. Remember that."

"And the kid and the girl got into the jeep like two little lambs, just like that? And they just drove off?" The lieutenant couldn't believe it, judging by the expression on his face. Lituma didn't believe it either.

"She didn't want to, she didn't trust them, and tried to stop him: Let's stay right here. Don't believe him, don't believe him."

"Come on now, let's get going, my dear," the voice of the older one encouraged them from the jeep. "He's a deserter, don't forget. He has to go back. This has to be taken care of immediately. This black mark has to be erased from his service record. He's got to think of his future. Let's get going."

"Yes, dear, he's right, he's forgiven us, let's do what he wants and get in. I believe what he says. He wouldn't lie."

"He wouldn't lie." Lituma felt a tear run down his cheek to his lips. It was salty, a drop of sea water. He kept on hearing Doña Lupe, her voice as deep as the ocean, interrupted from time to time by the lieutenant's questions. He vaguely understood that she was no longer telling anything she hadn't already said about the matter they had come to investigate. She cursed her bad luck, she wondered what would happen to her, she asked heaven what sin she'd committed that she should be tangled up in this horrible story. At times she sobbed. But nothing she said interested Lituma.

It was a kind of waking dream, again and again he saw the happy couple enjoying their premarital honeymoon in the humble streets of Amotape: he a half-breed *cholo* from Castilla; she a white girl of good family. There are no barriers to love, as the old waltz said. In this case the song was correct: love had broken through social and racial prejudices, as well as the economic abyss that separated the two lovers. The love they must have felt for each other had to have been intense, uncontrollable, to make them do what they did. "I've never felt a love like that, not even that time I fell in love with Meche, Josefino's girl." No, he'd fallen in love a couple of times, but they were passing fancies that faded if the woman gave in or if she put up such a strong resistance that he finally got bored. But he'd never felt a love so powerful he'd risk his life for it, the kind the kid had felt, the kind that had made the girl stand up to the whole world. "Maybe I'm not the kind who gets to feel real love," he thought. "Probably it's because I've spent my life chasing whores with the Unstoppables, my heart's turned whore, and now I can't love a woman the way the kid did."

"What am I going to do now, sir?" he heard Doña Lupe implore. "Give me some advice, at least."

The lieutenant, already standing, asked how much he owed her for the *chicha* and the stewed kid. When the woman said it was on the house, he insisted. He wasn't, he said, one of those parasitic cops who abused their power, he paid his own way, on or off duty.

"But at least tell me what I should do now." She had her palms pressed together as if she were praying. "They're going to kill me, the way they killed that poor kid. Don't you see that? I don't know where to go. I have no place to go. Didn't I cooperate the way you asked? Tell me what I should do now."

"Just stay quiet, Doña Lupe." The lieutenant put the money for the meal next to the *chicha* gourd. "No one's going to kill you. No one will even bother you. Just go on living your normal life and forget what you saw, what you heard, and what you told us. Take it easy, now." He flicked the visor of his cap with his fingers, his usual way of saying goodbye. Lituma got up quickly and followed him out, forgetting to bid Doña Lupe farewell.

Walking out into the open air and receiving the vertical sun full blast without the protection of the woven mats and bamboo poles was like walking into hell. Within a few

seconds, he felt his khaki shirt soaked and his head throbbing. Lieutenant Silva was stepping along smartly, while
Lituma's boots were sinking into the sand, making each
step an effort. They walked up the winding main street of
Amotape toward the open land and the highway.

As they walked along, Lituma glimpsed the clusters of
human eyes behind the bamboo walls of the shacks, Doña
Lupe's curious, nervous neighbors. When he and the lieutenant arrived, they'd all hidden, because they were frightened of the police. As soon as they were out of sight, Lituma
was sure they'd all run over to Doña Lupe's cabin to ask
what happened, what the cops had seen and said. Lituma
and the lieutenant walked in silence, each deep in his own
thoughts.

As they were passing the last houses, a mangy dog ran
out to snarl at them. When they reached the sandy ground,
darting lizards appeared and disappeared among the rocks.
Lituma thought there were probably foxes as well as lizards.
The kids had probably heard them howling during the two
days they'd found refuge in Amotape. The foxes probably
came in at night to prowl around the corrals where the
goats and chickens were kept. Would the girl have been
frightened when she heard the howling? Would she have
hugged him close, trembling, seeking protection? Would
he have calmed her down whispering sweet words into her
ear? Or would they have been so in love that they would
be oblivious, so absorbed in each other that they wouldn't
even hear the noises of the world? Had they made love for
the first time in Amotape? Or had they done it among the
sand dunes surrounding the Piura Air Force Base?

When they reached the edge of the highway, Lituma was soaked from head to foot, as if he'd jumped fully clothed into a stream. He saw that Lieutenant Silva's green trousers and cream-colored shirt also had large dark patches and that his forehead was covered with beads of sweat. There wasn't a vehicle of any kind in sight. The lieutenant shrugged his shoulders in a gesture of resignation: "We'll have to be patient." He took out a pack of Incas, offered a cigarette to Lituma, and lit one for himself. For a while they smoked in silence, baking in the heat, thinking, observing the mirage of lakes, fountains, and seas out in front of them on the endless sand. The first truck that passed going toward Talara didn't stop, despite the frantic gestures both made with their hats.

"On my first tour of duty, in Abancay, when I'd just graduated from officer candidate school, I had a boss who wouldn't stand for bullshit like that. A captain who, if anyone ever did something like that, you know what he did, Lituma? He'd take out his revolver and blow out the guy's tires." The lieutenant stared bitterly at the truck disappearing in the distance. "We called him Captain Cunthound because he was always after women. Wouldn't you like to blow out that bastard's tires?"

"Yes, Lieutenant."

The officer looked at him curiously.

"You can't get all that stuff you heard out of your head, can you?"

Lituma nodded.

"I just can't believe everything Doña Lupe told us. Or that it happened here in this miserable hole."

The lieutenant tossed his cigarette butt to the other side of the road and mopped his forehead and neck with his already drenched handkerchief.

"Right. She told us a lot."

"I never thought the story would turn out like this, Lieutenant. I'd imagined all kinds of things, but not this."

"Does that mean that you know everything that happened to the kid, Lituma?"

"Well, more or less, Lieutenant. Don't you?"

"Not yet. That's another thing you're going to have to learn. Nothing's easy, Lituma. The truths that seem most truthful, if you look at them from all sides, if you look at them close up, turn out either to be half truths or lies."

"Okay, that may be, but in this case, aren't things pretty much cut-and-dried?"

"As of now, even though you think I'm kidding, I'm not even completely convinced that it was Colonel Mindreau and Lieutenant Dufó who killed him." There was no irony in his voice. "The only thing I'm sure of is that they were the two men who came here and took them away."

"I'm going to tell you something. That's not what got to me in all this. Know what it is? Now I know why the kid enlisted at the Talara base. So he could be near the girl he loved. Doesn't it seem incredible that anyone would do something like that? That a boy exempt from the draft would come and join up for love, to be near the girl he loves?"

"And why does that surprise you so much?" said Lieutenant Silva, laughing.

"It's certainly not what just anybody would do, not something you hear of every day."

Lieutenant Silva began to flag down a vehicle approaching in the distance.

"Then you don't know what love is. I'd join the Air Force, become a buck private in the Army, become a priest, a garbageman, and I'd even eat shit if I had to, just to be near my chubby, Lituma."

6

"THERE SHE IS. Didn't I tell you? Here she comes," exclaimed Lieutenant Silva, his binoculars jammed against his eyes. He stretched his neck like a giraffe reaching for a high branch. "As punctual as if she were meeting the Queen of England for tea. Welcome, my dear! Come on, strip so we can see you once and for all. Get down, Lituma, if she even turns this way a little she'll see us for sure."

Lituma flattened out behind the rock where they'd taken up positions half an hour earlier. Was that dust cloud approaching them really Doña Adriana? Or was Lieutenant Silva so hot for her that he was seeing visions? The two of them were hiding up on Crab Point, a natural watchtower that overlooked a stony beach and a quiet inlet. How had the lieutenant discovered that Doña Adriana came here to take her afternoon baths when the setting sun turned red and the heat relented a little? Because in fact that moving red dust cloud was Doña Adriana. Lituma could now make out her compact shape and undulating walk.

"This is the greatest gift I've ever given anyone, Lituma. You're going to see Chubby's ass, nothing less. And her tits. And, if you're lucky, her snatch with its curly little hairs. Get ready, Lituma, because you're going to die when you see it all. It's your birthday present, your promotion. How lucky you are to work for a guy like me!"

Lieutenant Silva had been chattering like a parrot ever since they'd arrived, but Lituma barely heard him. He paid more attention to the crabs than to his boss's jokes or even to the advent of Doña Adriana. The point was justifiably famous for its myriad crabs: each one of those tiny holes in the ground represented a crab. Lituma watched in fascination as they peeked out, looking at first like moving stains. Once they emerged, they stretched, widened, and began to run in that confusing way which made it impossible to know if they were moving forward or backward. "Just like us in this Palomino Molero business."

"Get down, get down, don't let her see you. Terrific! She's stripping."

It occurred to Lituma that the entire point was honey-combed with crab tunnels. What if it caved in? Both of them would sink into the dark, asphyxiating sand crawling with swarms of those living shells armed with pincers. Before they died, they'd suffer hellish torture. He patted the ground: it was as hard as stone. Good.

"Well, at least lend me the binoculars," Lituma complained. "You invited me here so I could see her, too, but you're doing all the looking."

"Why do you think I'm the boss, asshole?" But he passed him the binoculars. "Take a quick look. I don't want you to become an addict."

Lituma adjusted the binoculars and looked. He saw Doña Adriana down below, leaning against the breakwater, calmly taking off her dress. Did she know she was being watched? Did she take her time like that just to get the lieutenant hot and bothered? No, her movements were loose and casual, because she was sure she was alone. She folded her dress and stretched to lay it on a rock where the spray wouldn't reach it. Just as the lieutenant had said, she wore a short pink slip, and Lituma could see her thighs, which were as thick as young laurel trees, and her breasts, which were exposed right to the edge of her nipples.

"Who would have thought that at her age Doña Adriana had so many tasty little tidbits?"

"Don't look so hard. You're going to wear her out," the lieutenant scolded him as he took back the binoculars. "Actually, the best part comes now when she goes in the water, because the slip sticks to her body and turns transparent. This is not a show for enlisted men, Lituma. Only lieutenants and above."

Lituma laughed, just to be amiable, not because the lieutenant's jokes were funny. He felt uncomfortable and impatient. Was it because of Palomino Molero? Could be. Ever since he'd seen the boy impaled, crucified, and burned on that rocky field, he hadn't been able to get him out of his mind for a single moment. At first he thought that once they'd found out who killed him and why, he'd be free of Palomino Molero. But now, even though they'd more or less cleared up the mystery, the image of the boy was in his mind night and day. You're ruining my life, you little bastard. He decided that this weekend he'd ask the lieutenant for a pass to go to Piura. It was payday. He'd dig up the Unstoppables and invite them to get drunk at La

Chunga's place. Then they'd finish off the evening in the Green House, with the whores. That would get his mind off things and make him feel better, goddamn it.

"My little Chubby belongs to a superior race of women: those who don't wear panties. Think of all the advantages of having a woman who goes through life without panties."

Lieutenant Silva passed him the binoculars, but no matter how much he squinted, he really didn't see very much. Doña Adriana bathed right at the edge of the water: her paddling and the mild surf made her slip wet and translucent, so Lituma could actually see her body. It was garbage.

"My eyes must not be so good, or maybe I just don't have your imagination, Lieutenant. All I see is foam."

"Go fuck yourself. I, on the other hand, can see her as if she were on display. From top to bottom, from back to front. And, if you're at all interested, I can tell you that her pubic hair's as curly as any black woman's. I can tell you how many hairs she has, if you want to know. I see them so clearly I can count them one by one."

"And what else?" said the girl, standing behind them.

Lituma fell over backward. At the same time, he twisted his head so sharply that he wrenched his neck. Even though he could see it wasn't so, he kept thinking it wasn't a woman who had spoken but a crab.

"What else can you add to the list of obscenities you've already spit out?" She had her fists on her hips, like a matador challenging a bull. "What other disgusting expressions do you have in your filthy mind? Are there any more left in the dictionary, or have I heard them all? I've also been watching the dirty way you've been looking at her. You make me sick to my stomach."

Lieutenant Silva bent over to pick up his binoculars, which he'd dropped when the girl spoke. Lituma, still sitting on the ground, vaguely convinced he'd smashed an empty crab shell when he fell, saw that his boss had not yet recovered from the shock. He shook the sand off his trousers to gain a little time. He saluted, and Lituma heard him say: "It's dangerous to surprise the police when they're involved in their work, miss. Suppose I'd turned around shooting?"

"*Their work?* You call spying on women while they bathe your work?"

It was only then that Lituma realized she was Colonel Mindreau's daughter. That's right, Alicia Mindreau. His heart pounded in his chest. Now, from down below, boomed the outraged voice of Doña Adriana. Because of all the noise, she'd discovered them. As if in a dream, Lituma saw her stumble out of the water and run, half crouched and covering herself with her hands.

"You're not only pigs, but you abuse your authority, too. You call yourselves policemen? You're even worse than what people say the cops are."

"This point is a natural lookout. We use it to keep track of boats bringing in contraband from Ecuador," said the lieutenant with such conviction in his voice that Lituma's jaw fell open as he listened. "Besides, miss, in case you didn't already know it, insults from a lady like you are like roses to a gentleman. So go right ahead if it makes you feel better."

Out of the corner of his eye, Lituma could see that Doña Adriana, half dressed, was bustling down the beach toward Punta Arena. She was swinging her hips, moving along energetically, and even though her back was to them, she was making furious gestures. She was probably cursing them up and down. The girl had fallen silent and stared at them as if her fury and disgust had suddenly abated. She was covered with grime from head to toe. It was impossible to know what the original color of her sleeveless blouse or her jeans had been because they were both the same dull ocher tone of the surrounding sand flats.

To Lituma she seemed even thinner than on the day he'd seen her burst into Colonel Mindreau's office. Flat-chested, with narrow hips, she was what Lieutenant Silva mockingly called a board member. That pretentious nose, which seemed to grade people according to their smell, seemed even haughtier to him than the previous time. She sniffed at them as if they had failed her olfactory test. Was she sixteen? Eighteen?

"What's a nice young lady like you doing among all these crabs?" Lieutenant Silva had slyly consigned the Peeping Tom incident to oblivion. He put his binoculars back into their case and began to clean his sunglasses with his handkerchief. "This is a bit far from the base for a stroll, isn't it? Suppose some animal took a bite out of you? What happened to you? Get a flat?"

Lituma found Alicia Mindreau's bicycle about sixty feet below, at the foot of Crab Point. Like its owner, it was covered with dirt. He studied the girl and tried to imagine Palomino Molero standing next to her. They'd be holding hands, saying tender things to each other, staring dreamily into each other's eyes. She, fluttering her eyelids like butter-flies, would whisper in his ear: "Sing to me, please, sing something pretty." No. He couldn't. He just could not imagine them like that.

"My dad knows you've been getting things out of Ricardo," she said suddenly in a cutting tone. She had her face tilted up and her eyes were measuring the effect her words had on them. "You took advantage of him when he was drunk the other night."

The lieutenant didn't bat an eye. He carefully put on his sunglasses and began to descend the point toward the path, sliding on his backside as if on a sled. When he was down, he slapped the dust off his clothes.

"Is Lieutenant Dufó's first name really Ricardo? His friends love the gringos so much that they probably call him Richard."

"Daddy also knows you went to Amotape to talk to Doña Lupe." She was actually rather short, small, barely any figure at all. She was no beauty. Did Palomino Molero fall in love with her just because of who she was? "He knows everything you've been doing."

Why did she talk like this? Alicia Mindreau didn't seem to be threatening them; instead, she seemed to be making fun of them, turning them into the object of some private joke. Now Lituma came scrambling down the point, right behind the girl. The crabs zigzagged back and forth between his legs. There was no one in sight. The men in charge of the oil tanks must have left a while ago because the gates were locked and there was no noise on the other side.

They had reached the path that led from the point to

the fence that separated the I.P.C. from Talara. The lieutenant took the bicycle and pushed it along with one hand.
They walked slowly, in Indian file, the crab shells crunch-
ing under their feet.

"I followed you from your headquarters and neither of
you realized it," she said in the same unpredictable tone,
mixing anger and mockery. "At the gate there, they tried to
stop me, but I threatened to tell my daddy and they let
me pass. You two didn't even hear me. I was listening to
you say all those dirty things and you didn't even know I
was there. If I hadn't spoken, I could still be there spying
on you."

The lieutenant agreed, laughing quietly. He moved his
head from one side to the other in mock shame, congratulating her.

"When men are by themselves, they talk dirty. We came
to see what was going on, to see if any smugglers were
around. It's not our fault if some Talara ladies came to
bathe at the same time. A coincidence, right, Lituma?"

"Yes, Lieutenant."

"In any case, Miss Mindreau, we're at your service. What
can we do for you? Or would you prefer we talk over at the
office? In the shade, and drinking sodas, we can be more
comfortable. Naturally, our little office is not as comfortable as your dad's."

The girl said nothing. Lituma could feel his thick, dark
red blood coursing slowly through his veins and his pulse
pounding in his wrists and temples. They went through the
gate, and the Guardia Civil on duty, Lucio Tinoco from
Huancabamba, gave the lieutenant a military salute. There
were also three guards from International's own security

force on duty. They gaped at the girl, surprised to see her
with Lieutenant Silva and Lituma. Were people in town
already gossiping about their trip to Amotape? It wasn't
Lituma's fault. He had scrupulously followed his boss's
order to say nothing about Doña Lupe.

They passed the shiny green company hospital, then the
harbor officer's headquarters, where two sailors stood guard
with rifles on their shoulders. One of them winked at
Lituma and nodded toward the lieutenant and the girl, as
if to say birds of a feather flock together.

"Does Colonel Mindreau know you've come to see us?"

"Don't be a fool. Of course he doesn't know."

"He'll find out soon enough," thought Lituma. Everyone
looked surprised to see the three of them together. Then
they stared and whispered to each other.

"Did you come just to tell us that the colonel found out
we'd had a chat with Lieutenant Dufó and with Doña
Lupe?" He spoke looking straight ahead, not turning toward
Alicia Mindreau, and Lituma, who had dropped back a
bit, could see that she also kept her head facing forward,
never looking at the lieutenant.

"That's right."

"A lie," Lituma thought. What had she come to tell
them? Had the colonel sent her? In any case, she seemed
to be having trouble speaking. Maybe she'd lost her nerve.
Her brow was furrowed, her mouth half open, and her
arrogant little nose twitched anxiously. Her skin was very
white and her eyelashes extremely long. Was it her air of
delicacy, fragility, of being a pampered child, that drove
the kid wild? Whatever it was she'd come to tell them, she
was sorry now and would say nothing.

"It certainly was nice of you to drop by and chat with us. Really, thanks a lot."

They walked on in silence fifty yards or so, listening to the cries of the sea gulls and the roar of the surf. At one of the wooden houses, some women were expertly cleaning fish. Around them, snarling and jumping, was a pack of dogs, waiting to devour the waste. The stench was overpowering.

"What was Palomino Molero like, miss?" A chill ran down Lituma's spine, he was so surprised to hear himself. He'd spoken without premeditation, point-blank. Neither the lieutenant nor the girl turned to look at him. Now Lituma walked just behind them, occasionally stumbling.

"The nicest boy in the world. An angel come from heaven."

Her voice did not tremble with bitterness or nostalgia as she spoke. Neither did it express tenderness. It was that same unusual tone, something between innocence and sarcasm, in which there occasionally flashed a spark of rage.

"That's exactly what everyone who knew him says," murmured Lituma, when the silence began to seem too long. "That he was a really nice guy."

"You must have suffered a great deal because of Palomino Molero's tragedy, Miss Alicia," said the officer after a moment. "Isn't that so?"

Alicia Mindreau said nothing. They were passing a cluster of houses under construction, some without roofs, others with walls half finished. There were old men in T-shirts sitting on their front porches, naked children collecting shells, and knots of women. The air echoed with laughter, and the smell of fish was everywhere.

Lituma made yet another spontaneous remark: "My friends say I heard him sing one time in Piura, but no matter how I try, I can't remember. They say his specialty was boleros."

"And folk songs, too," she added, nodding energetically. "He could also play the guitar really well."

"That's right, the guitar. His mother, Doña Asunta, from Castilla, is a little crazy on the subject of her son's guitar. She wants to get it back. Who could have stolen it?"

"I have it," said Alicia Mindreau. Her voice broke suddenly, as if she hadn't meant to say the words she'd just spoken.

Again, the three of them were silent. They were heading toward the heart of Talara, and the more deeply they moved into the tangle of houses, the more people there were crowding the streets. Behind the fences, on the point where the lighthouse was located and on Punta Arena, where the gringos and executives of the I.P.C. had their houses, the streetlights had already been turned on, though the sun was still shining. This was also true up above the cliffs, on the air base. At one end of the bay, the oil refinery spewed out a plume of reddish-gold flame; the structure looked like a gigantic crab dangling its legs in the water.

"The poor old lady said, *When they find the guitar, they'll find the killers.* Not that she knows anything. Pure women's or mothers' intuition."

He felt the lieutenant turn to look at him.

"What's she like?" said the girl. Now she turned, and for a second Lituma saw her face: dirty, pale, irascible, and curious.

"Do you mean Doña Asunta, Palomino Molero's mother?"

"Is she a *chola*, a half-breed?" specified the girl impatiently.

It seemed to Lituma that his boss guffawed.

"Well, she's just an ordinary woman. Just like all these people around here, just like me," he heard himself say, and was surprised at how annoyed he was with her. "Of course, she doesn't belong to the same class as you or Colonel Mindreau. Is that what you wanted to know?"

"He didn't look like a *cholo*," said Alicia Mindreau in a softer tone, as if talking to herself. "His hair was very fine, even blondish. And he had the best manners of any man I've ever known. Not even Ricardo or my father have manners like his. No one would have believed he'd gone to public school or that he was from Castilla. The only thing *cholo* about him was his name, Palomino. And his second name was even worse, Temístocles."

Again it seemed to Lituma that his boss had laughed. But he didn't have the slightest desire to laugh at what the girl was saying. He was puzzled and intrigued. Was she sorry or angry at the boy's death? There was no way to guess. The colonel's daughter talked as though Palomino Molero hadn't been killed in the horrible way they all knew he had, as if he were still alive. Could she be a bit crazy?

"Where did you meet Palomino Molero?" asked Lieutenant Silva.

They had reached the rear of the church. That was the white wall that Teotonio Calle Frías used as the screen for his portable outdoor movie house. Those who wanted to sit down to see the movie had to bring their own chairs, but most people just hunkered down or stretched out on the ground. To get a good view, you had to pay five reales, which allowed you to sit, crouch, or recline on the other side of a rope. The lieutenant and Lituma could always get in free. Those who didn't want to pay could always watch the movie free from outside the roped-off area. Of course, the view was bad and gave you a sore neck.

Many people had already taken up positions and were waiting for it to get dark. Don Teotonio Calle Frías was setting up his projector. He had only one, which worked thanks to a wire he himself had run to the power line on the corner. After each reel, there was an interruption while the next was loaded. The movies, accordingly, were strung out in pieces and were extremely long. Even so, the improvised theater was always full, especially in summer. "Ever since the kid's murder, I haven't been to the movies once," thought Lituma. What was on tonight? A Mexican movie likely as not. Yes, *Hidden River*, starring Dolores del Río and Columba Domínguez.

"I met him at Lala Mercado's birthday party over in Piura." She'd taken so long to answer that Lituma forgot which question she was answering. "He'd been hired to sing at the party. All the girls were saying how beautifully he sang, what a pretty voice, how good-looking he is, he doesn't look like a *cholo*. It's true he didn't."

"These damned whites." Lituma was indignant.

"And did he dedicate any songs to you, miss?" The lieutenant oozed respect for her. Periodically, Lituma realized, his boss revealed yet another interrogation tactic; this one combined infinite respect with extraordinary politeness.

"Three. 'The Last Night We Spent Together,' 'Moonbeam,' and 'Pretty Baby.'"

"She's not normal; she's off her rocker," Lituma decided. Alicia Mindreau's bicycle, which the lieutenant was pulling with his left hand, had begun to screech intermittently. The recurring, piercing sound put Lituma's nerves on edge.

"We danced together, too. Just once. He danced with all the girls once. But twice with Lala Mercado—because it was her party, not because he liked her more. Nobody thought it was wrong for him to dance with us. In fact, we all wanted to dance with him. He behaved just like one of us. And he was a terrific dancer."

Just like one of us, thought Lituma, carefully stepping over a dried-out starfish covered with ants. "Would Alicia Mindreau think of Lieutenant Silva as 'one of us'? Not me, of course. I'm a purebred *cholo*," he thought. "From La Mangachería, and proud of it." He had his eyes half closed and he wasn't seeing how Talara's afternoon was quickly giving way to night. He was seeing the party and the garden, all the well-dressed young couples over in that whites-only part of town near the sand flats by La Chunga's place on Buenos Aires Street. Lala Mercado's house. He was seeing a couple dancing in a corner, staring into each other's eyes, speaking only with their eyes: Alicia Mindreau and Palomino. No, it was impossible. And yet she was the one telling the story:

"When we started dancing, he told me that the moment

he saw me he'd fallen in love with me." Not even now was there a note of sadness in her voice. She was speaking quickly, without emotion, as if dictating a message. "He told me he'd always believed in love at first sight and that now he knew it was real. Because he'd fallen in love with me right then and there. He said I could laugh at him if I wanted, but that it was the truth. He'd never love another woman in his life. He said that even if I told him to get lost, even if I spit on him and treated him like a dog, that he'd go on loving me until the day he died."

"He kept his word, too," thought Lituma. Was she crying? Not a chance. Lituma couldn't see her face—he was still one step behind the lieutenant and the girl—but her voice was dry, unwavering, severe in the extreme. At the same time, it was as if she were talking about someone else and not herself, as if what she was saying had nothing to do with her, as if there were no blood and murder in her tale.

"He said he'd come over and serenade me. That if he sang to me every night, he'd make me fall in love with him," she went on after a short pause. The rhythmic screech of the bicycle made Lituma feel an inexplicable anguish; he waited for it to come, and when it did, a chill ran through his entire body. He listened to the lieutenant chirping away like a little bird perched on Alicia Mindreau's shoulder:

"Did it really happen like that? Was that the way it was? Did he keep his word? Did he really come over to the Piura Air Force Base and serenade you at your house? And did you end up falling in love with him?"

"I don't know."

"She *doesn't know*? How can she not know that?" Lituma
searched his own memory for the time when he'd been
most deeply in love. Was it with Meche, Josefino's girl, a
statuesque blonde for whom he'd never dared to make a
play? Sure, he'd been in love that time. How can you not
know if you're in love? How dumb can you get? Which
means she's nuts. Or was she just playing dumb to screw
them up? Could the colonel have taught her how to act
like that? He couldn't decide.

"But Palomino Molero did serenade you over at the Air
Force base in Piura, didn't he? Did he do it often?"

"Every day. Starting the night after Lala Mercado's party.
He never missed once, until Daddy was transferred over
here."

"And what did your dad say about those serenades?"
chirped the lieutenant. "Did he ever catch him at it?"

"My father knew he was serenading me, what do you
think he is, deaf?" It seemed to Lituma that Alicia
Mindreau was vacillating, as if she had been about to say
something and then was sorry she'd thought of it.

"What did he say about it?"

"That for Palomino I had to be something special, the
Queen of England," stated the girl in her dead-serious voice.
"When I told Palito about it, he told me Daddy was wrong,
that I was much more than the Queen of England for him,
that I was more like the Virgin Mary."

For the third time, Lituma was sure he'd heard Lieutenant Silva's mocking little laugh. "*Palito*? Was that her
pet name for him? Which meant that Palito was an okay
name, but Palomino or Temístocles were *cholo* names.
Damn but these whites are complicated people."

They'd reached the Guardia Civil station. The man on duty, Ramiro Matelo, from Chiclayo, had abandoned his post, shutting the office door behind him. Lieutenant Silva used the bicycle as a doorstop to keep it open.

"Come on in and rest awhile," invited the lieutenant, making a half bow. "We can offer you a soda or a cup of coffee. Please come in."

Night had fallen. As Lituma and Lieutenant Silva lit the paraffin lamps, they bumped into each other and into the office furniture. The girl waited calmly by the door. No, her eyes had no tears in them. Lituma saw her slim shadow appear against the bulletin board where they pinned up reports and the orders of the day, and thought about Palomino Molero. He was afraid, panicky. "I can't believe this is happening to me." Did that immobile little thing over there really tell them all that stuff about Palomino Molero? He was seeing her, but at the same time it was as if the girl were not there and had said nothing, as if it was all a figment of his imagination.

"I hope our little hike didn't tire you out." The lieutenant was lighting the camp stove, on which there was always a full kettle of water. "Get the young lady a chair, Lituma."

Alicia Mindreau sat on the edge of the chair, with her back to the door and the lamp closest to it. Her face was half in shadow and her silhouette was surrounded by a yellow haze. She looked even more like a child. Could she still be in high school? In one of the neighboring houses they were frying something. In the distance, a drunken voice was singing about the city of Paita.

"What are you waiting for, Lituma? Get the young lady a soda."

Lituma rushed to get a Pasteurina out of the pail of water that kept their soda supply cool. He opened it and offered it to her, excusing himself: "I'm sorry but we don't have any straws or glasses. I'm afraid you'll have to drink straight from the bottle."

She took the Pasteurina and raised it to her mouth as if she were a robot. Was she nuts? Or was she suffering inside and couldn't show it? Did she seem so strange because she was trying to cover up? Lituma thought she looked hypnotized. It was as if she didn't realize she was there with them, as if she had no idea what she'd told them. Lituma was embarrassed, uncomfortable seeing her so serious, so fixed and unmoving. He was frightened. Suppose the colonel turned up right now with a patrol to get even for this little chat with his daughter?

"Here, have a cup of coffee, too," said the lieutenant. He handed her the tin cup of instant coffee. "Sugar? One or two?"

"What's going to happen to my father?" she asked suddenly. There was no fear in her voice, just a trace of anger. "Will they throw him in jail? Will they shoot him?"

She'd put down the cup, and the lieutenant picked it up and took a long drink. Then Lituma watched him sit on the edge of his desk. Outside, the drunk was still babbling about the same subject, the stingrays in Paita bay. He said he'd been stung in the foot and was looking for a compassionate woman who'd suck out the poison.

"Nothing's going to happen to your father," said Lieutenant Silva. "Why should anything happen to him? They won't touch him. Don't worry about it, Miss Alicia. Sure you won't have some coffee? It looks like I've drunk this cup, but I can make another in a second."

"He knows every trick in the book. He could make a mute talk." Lituma had discreetly retreated to the wall. From there he could see the girl's oblique, thin profile, her solemn, judgmental little nose. Suddenly he understood Palomino: she certainly wasn't a beauty, but there was something in that cold face that was fascinating, mysterious, something that could drive a man crazy. He felt contradictory emotions. He wanted the lieutenant to get his way and make Alicia Mindreau tell everything she knew, but at the same time, without understanding why, he was sorry this child was going to reveal all her secrets. It was as if Alicia Mindreau were falling into a trap. He wanted to save her. Could she really be crazy?

"The one who might have a little trouble is the jealous lover." The lieutenant seemed almost sorry to have to mention it. "I mean Ricardo Dufó. Richard. Of course, jealousy is something that any judge who understands the human heart will call a mitigating circumstance. I mean, I always think of jealousy as a mitigating circumstance. If a guy really loves a woman, he gets jealous. I know it, miss, because I know what love is and I'm a jealous man. Jealousy upsets your thinking, keeps you from thinking straight. It's like drinking. If your boyfriend can prove that what he did to Palomino Molero happened because he was crazy—that's the important idea, miss, he's got to say he was crazy, remember that—it may be they'll say he wasn't responsible for his acts. With a little luck and a good lawyer, it may work out that way. So you needn't worry about your jealous lover either, Miss Mindreau."

He raised the cup to his lips and noisily drank the rest of the coffee. His forehead still had the mark of his cap, and Lituma could not see his eyes, hidden behind dark glasses. All he could see were the thin mustache, the mouth, and the chin. Once Lituma had asked him, "Why don't you ever take off your glasses, even when it's dark, Lieutenant?" He'd answered, mockingly, "So I can screw people up."

"I'm not worried about him. I hate him. I only wish the worst things in the world would happen to him. I say it to his face all the time. Once he went and got his revolver. He said to me, 'Just pull the trigger like this. Now take it. If you really hate me so much, I deserve to die. Do it, kill me.'"

There was a long silence, punctuated by the hiss of the frying pan in the house next door and the drunk's confused monologue. The drunk finally gave up and went off, saying that since nobody loved him around here he'd go see a witch he knew over in Ayabaca who'd cure his hurt foot.

"But I know in my heart that you're a good person who'd never kill anyone."

"Don't pretend to be dumber than you really are." Alicia Mindreau's chin was trembling, and her nostrils were flared. "Don't fool yourself into thinking I'm as dumb as you are. Please. I'm a grownup, after all."

"Please forgive me. I just didn't know what to say. What you said just caught me off-guard, really."

"So you actually don't know if you were in love with

Palomino Molero or not," Lituma heard himself mutter. "Didn't you come to love him, even a little bit?"

"Much more than a little bit," the girl quickly replied, again without turning in the direction of the enlisted man. Her head was still, and her rage seemed to have evaporated just as quickly as it had come. She stared into space. "I loved Palito a lot. If we had found the priest in Amotape, I would have married him. But what you call falling in love is disgusting, and what we had was beautiful. Are you playing dumb, too?"

"What kind of question is that to ask, Lituma?" Lituma understood that the lieutenant wasn't really reproaching him, that it was all part of his plan to keep the girl talking. "Do you think that if the young lady didn't love him she would have eloped with him? Or do you think he kidnapped her?"

Alicia Mindreau said nothing. More and more insects buzzed around the paraffin lamps. Now they could hear the tide as it came in. The fishermen were probably setting up their nets. Don Matías Querecotillo and his two helpers were probably pushing *The Lion of Talara* into the surf, or they might already be rowing beyond the floating piers. He wished he were there with them instead of here listening to these things. And, nevertheless, he heard himself whisper: "And what about your other boyfriend, miss?" As he spoke, he felt he was balancing on a high wire.

"You must mean Miss Mindreau's official boyfriend," said the lieutenant, correcting Lituma. He sweetened his tone as he spoke to her: "Because since you came to love Palomino Molero, I would imagine that Lieutenant Dufó could only be a kind of screen to keep up appearances in front of your father. That's how it was, right?"

"That's right."

"So your dad wouldn't catch on about your love for Palomino Molero. Naturally, it wouldn't exactly make your father happy to find out his daughter was in love with an ordinary airman."

Lituma's nerves were put on edge now by the buzzing insects smashing against the lamps, in the same way they'd been put on edge before by the screeching bicycle.

"He enlisted just so he could be near you?" Lituma realized that this time he was no longer faking: his voice was saturated with the immense pity he felt for the kid. What had he seen in this half-crazy girl? That she was from a good family, that she was white? Or did her rapidly changing moods fascinate him, those incredible passions that in a few seconds made her pass from fury to indifference?

"The poor jealous guy couldn't understand a bit of this," the lieutenant was thinking out loud as he lit a cigarette. "But when he did figure a few things out, he went nuts. That's it: he lost control of himself. He did what he felt he had to do, and then, half crazy with fear, sorry for what had happened, he came to you. Crying his eyes out, he must have said, *Alicita, I'm a murderer. I tortured and killed the airman you ran away with.* You confessed that you never loved him, that you hated him. And then he brought you his revolver and said, *Kill me.* But you didn't do it. First you cheated on him, then he took it on the neck. Poor Richard Dufó. On top of that, the colonel forbade him to see you ever again. Because naturally a son-in-law who's a

murderer is just as socially unacceptable as a little *cholo*
from Castilla—a common airman at that. Poor jealous
Richard! Well, that seems to be the whole story. Was I
wrong about anything, miss?"

"Ha-ha! You were wrong about every single thing!"

"I know. I said it that way on purpose. Tell me how it
really was."

Did she really laugh? Yes, a short little laugh, ferociously
mocking. Now she was serious again, sitting stiffly on the
edge of her chair with her knees together. Her little arms
were so thin that Lituma could have wrapped his fingers
around both of them at the same time. Sitting there half in
the shadow, her body so tall and slender, she could have
been taken for a boy. And yet she was a young woman.
No longer a virgin. He tried to imagine her naked, trembling
in Palomino Molero's arms, lying on a cot in Amotape, or
maybe on a straw mat in the sand. Wrapping her little arms
around Palomino's neck, opening her mouth, spreading her
legs, moaning. No, impossible. He couldn't see her. In the
interminable pause that followed, the buzz of insects became deafening.

"The one who brought me the revolver and told me to
kill him was Daddy. What will you do to him?"

"Nothing," stuttered Lieutenant Silva, as if he were
choking. "Nobody's going to lay a hand on your dad."

"There's no justice. He should be thrown in jail, killed.
But no one would dare to. Of course, who'd dare to do it?"

Lituma had stiffened. He could feel that the lieutenant
was also tense, panting, as if they were hearing the rumble
that comes from the bowels of the earth just before a
tremor.

"I want to drink something hot, that coffee if there's nothing else," said the girl, once again changing her tone. Now she was talking without dramatics, as if chatting with her friends. "I think I'm cold!"

"That's because it is cold," blurted out the lieutenant. He repeated himself twice, nodding his head and making other superfluous gestures. "It is cold, it certainly is."

He hesitated awhile, finally stood up and walked to the stove, Lituma noticed how awkward and slow he was; he moved as if he were drunk. Now it was he who was taken by surprise, jolted by what he'd just heard. Lituma pulled himself together and began to think again about what had bothered him most: what was all this about love being disgusting and then she'd fallen in love with Palomino Molero? What kind of nutty idea was that? Falling in love was disgusting but loving someone wasn't? Lituma, too, felt cold. How great it would be to have a nice hot cup of coffee, like the one the lieutenant was making for the girl. Through the cone of greenish light that fell from the lamp, Lituma could see how slowly the lieutenant was pouring out the water, how slowly he stirred in the instant coffee and the sugar. It was as if he weren't sure that his fingers would do his bidding. In silence he walked toward the girl, holding the cup with two hands, and then handed it to her. Alicia Mindreau instantly raised it to her lips and drank, turning her face upward. Lituma saw her eyes in the fragile, shimmering light: dry, black, hard, and adult, set in the delicate face of a child.

"In that case . . ." murmured the lieutenant, so slowly that Lituma could barely hear him. He'd again perched on the corner of his desk, with one leg on the floor and the other dangling in midair. He paused and then went on timidly, "In that case, the one you hate, the one you hope suffers the worst things, is not Lieutenant Dufó but . . ."

He didn't dare finish the sentence. Lituma saw the girl nod without hesitation.

"He gets down on the floor like a dog and kisses my feet. He says love knows no bounds. The world wouldn't understand. Blood calls to blood, he says. Love is love, a landslide that carries all before it. When he says those things, when he does those things, when he cries and asks me to forgive him, I hate him. I only wish the worst things would happen to him."

A radio turned up full blast silenced her. The disk jockey spoke machine-gun style, whining through the static. Lituma couldn't understand a word he said. The disk jockey's voice drowned out by a popular dance, *el bote,* which was usurping the place of the *huaracha* among the citizens of Talara:

Look at all those chicks standin' on the corner,
They don' pay me no mind, even though they oughta . . .

Lituma was enraged by the singer, by the person who'd turned on the radio, by *el bote,* and even by himself. "That's why she says it's disgusting. That's why she makes a distinction between falling in love and loving someone." The long pause in the conversation was filled in by the music. Again Alicia Mindreau seemed calm, her fury of an instant ago forgotten. Her little head moved in time with *el bote* as she looked at the lieutenant expectantly.

"I've just realized something," he heard his boss announce, very slowly.

The girl stood up and declared, "I have to be going. It's quite late."

"I've just realized that it was you who left the anonymous note on our door. It was you who advised us to go to Amotape to ask Doña Lupe what happened to Palomino Molero."

"They must be looking everywhere for me." In her little voice, again transformed, Lituma discovered that mischievous and mocking tone which was her most likable or least unlikable characteristic. When she talked like that, she seemed to be really what she was, a child, and not, as a moment before, a grownup, terrible woman with the face and body of a child. "He's probably sent the chauffeur and the airmen to every house on the base, to the gringos' houses, to the club, to the movies, everywhere. He gets scared whenever I'm late. He thinks I'm going to run away again. Ha-ha!"

"So it was you. Well, it's a bit late, but thanks for your help, Miss Mindreau. If you hadn't given us that hint, we'd still be in a fog."

"The last place he'd ever think of looking is the police station. Ha-ha!"

Did she laugh? Yes, but this time with no sarcasm, no mockery. A rapid little laugh, roguish, like that of any kid on the street. She was crazy, no doubt about it. But Lituma was still plagued by doubts, and kept changing his mind. She was, she wasn't; of course she was; no, she was faking.

"Of course, of course," hummed the lieutenant. He coughed to clear his throat, tossed the butt of his cigarette on the floor, and stepped on it. "We're here to protect people. You most of all, of course. All you've got to do is ask."

"I don't need anyone to protect me. My daddy protects me. He's all I need."

She swiveled around toward the lieutenant so quickly that the few drops of coffee in the tin cup splashed all over his shirt. He snatched the cup out of her hands.

"Would you like us to escort you to the base?"

"No, I wouldn't." Lituma watched her walk swiftly out into the street. Her silhouette materialized in the twilight air as she got back on her bicycle. He watched her pedal off, heard a horn blow, and then saw her disappear, tracing a sinuous path around potholes and rocks.

Lieutenant Silva and Lituma stood stock-still. Now the music had stopped and once again they could hear the hideous voice of the announcer speaking in his incomprehensible staccato.

"If they hadn't turned on that fucking radio, she would have gone on talking," grunted Lituma. "God knows what else she would have told us."

"If we don't get a move on, Chubby's going to close the kitchen on us." The lieutenant stood up and put on his cap. "Let's get cracking, Lituma. Chow time. This stuff makes me hungry, how about you?"

Nonsense. Doña Adriana didn't close until midnight and it was barely eight o'clock. But Lituma understood that he'd said that just to say something, that he'd made a joke just to break the silence, because the lieutenant must have felt as strange and mixed up as he did. Lituma picked up the Pasteurina bottle Alicia Mindreau had left on the floor and tossed it into the sack of empties that Borrao Salinas, a rag-and-bottle man, would buy each weekend.

They walked out, locking the station door. The lieutenant muttered where the hell had the guard gone to, he'd punish Ramiro Matelo by restricting him to quarters on Saturday and Sunday. There was a full moon. The bluish light of the sky illuminated the street. They walked in silence, waving and nodding in response to the greetings shouted to them from the families congregated in doorways. Off in the distance, above the throbbing surf, they could hear the loudspeakers from the outdoor movie—Mexican voices, a woman weeping, background music.

"You must be shaken up after hearing all that, right?"

"Yes, Lieutenant, I am a little shaken up."

"Well, I told you you'd learn all kinds of weird things in this business."

"Truer words were never spoken, sir."

At the restaurant there were six regulars having dinner. They exchanged greetings with them, but the lieutenant and Lituma sat at a far-off table. Doña Adriana brought them some vegetable soup and fish, but instead of serving them, she more or less threw the dishes on the table, without answering their greeting. She was frowning, and when Lieutenant Silva asked if she was ill and why she was in such a foul mood, she barked out: "Would you mind explaining what you were doing on Crab Point this afternoon, wise guy?"

"I was informed that some smugglers were coming in," answered the lieutenant without blinking an eye.

"One day you're going to pay for all your little tricks, let me warn you."

"Thanks for the warning," said the lieutenant, smiling and puckering his lips obscenely to blow her a kiss. "Oh, maaaama!"

7

"MY FINGERS are all stiff, I've completely lost my touch. When I was a cadet, I could play any song I heard even once. Now I can't even scratch out 'La Raspa.' Shit."

Lieutenant Silva had in fact been trying several songs and they'd all come out flat. Lituma barely heard his boss because his mind was occupied by a single thought: what the fuck would happen now that they'd turned in a report like that?

They were on the fishermen's beach, between the two piers. It was after midnight: a blast from the refinery siren had just announced the new shift. Lituma and Lieutenant Silva were smoking a cigarette with old Matías Querecotillo, while his two helpers pushed *The Lion of Talara* into the surf. Doña Adriana's husband also wanted to find out if what people all over Talara were saying was true.

"And just what are people all over Talara saying, Don Matías?"

"That you two already know who killed Palomino Molero."

Lieutenant Silva told him what he told everyone who asked him that (although how the rumor had spread so quickly was still a mystery to him): "We can't say anything yet. Soon we'll tell what we know, Don Matías. I can tell you personally that the announcement's going to come any time now."

"I hope so, Lieutenant. I hope that, for once, justice is done and the people who always win find out what it's like to lose."

"Who do you mean, Don Matías?"

"Who else? You know as well as I do. The big guys."

He walked off, bouncing along like a bottle on the waves, and scrambled expertly onto his boat. He didn't act like a man who coughs up blood; he seemed robust and seaworthy for his age. Perhaps all that about his being sick was nothing more than Doña Adriana's imagination. Did Don Matías know that Lieutenant Silva was after his wife? He'd never shown it. Lituma noticed that the fisherman was always friendly to the lieutenant. Perhaps when you got old you stopped being jealous.

"The big guys . . . Do you think the big guys left this guitar on our doorstep as a gift for us?"

"No, Lieutenant. It was Colonel Mindreau's daughter. You yourself heard her say she had the kid's guitar."

"If you say so . . . but somehow I don't see it. I didn't see any letter or card or anything else that would prove she brought the guitar to the station. I don't even know for sure if this is Palomino Molero's guitar."

"Are you kidding me, Lieutenant?"

"No, Lituma. I'm trying to distract you a little because you're so edgy. Why are you so edgy? A Guardia Civil should have balls like a brass monkey."

"You're a bit jumpy yourself, sir. Don't try to deny it either."

Lieutenant Silva laughed involuntarily. "Of course I'm jumpy. But I cover it up so people can't see. You look as though you'd shit in your pants if you heard a mosquito fart."

The moon shone so brightly they could clearly see the outlines of the houses belonging to the gringos and the executives of the I.P.C., up on the cliff, near the blinking lighthouse. Everyone talked about how wonderful the Paita moon was, but the moon right here was the brightest and most perfectly round Lituma had ever seen. People should be talking about the moon of Talara. He imagined the kid on a night like this, singing right on this very beach, surrounded by captivated airmen:

> *Moon, moon*
> *Month of June*
> *Tell my baby*
> *I'll be back soon . . .*

Lituma and the lieutenant had gone to the movies and seen an Argentine film with Luis Sandrini which made everyone but them laugh. Then they had a talk with Father Domingo at the church door. The priest wanted a Guardia Civil to scare off the Don Juans who were molesting the Talara girls when they came for chorus rehearsals. Several mothers had withdrawn their daughters from chorus because of those wise guys. The lieutenant promised he would do it, provided, of course, he had a man available. When they got back to the station, they found the guitar the lieutenant now had on his knees. Someone had left it leaning against the door. Anyone could have taken it if they decided to have dinner instead of returning directly to the station. Lituma had no doubts about the significance of the guitar:

"She wants us to return it to the kid's mother. She felt sorry—maybe because of what I told her about Doña Asunta—and that's why she brought it."

"That may be what you think, but I don't buy it."

Why was the lieutenant always joking like that? Lituma knew very well that his boss was in no mood for laughter, that he had been uneasy ever since he sent in his report. The proof was that they were in the station at that hour of the night. After dinner, the lieutenant picked up the guitar and suggested they stretch their legs. They walked down to the fishermen's beach, in silence, each one immersed in his own worries. They watched the men prepare the nets and gear and then set sail.

Once they were alone, the lieutenant had started to strum Palomino's guitar. Perhaps he was too nervous to get a song out of it. That was it, even if he tried to hide it by telling jokes. For the first time since he'd begun to serve under him, Lituma hadn't heard him mention Doña Adriana even once. He was just about to ask him if he might bring the guitar to Doña Asunta the next time he went to Piura—"At least let me give this small consolation to the poor lady, Lieutenant"—when he realized they were no longer alone.

"Good evening," said the shadow.

He'd materialized suddenly, as if he'd sprung from the sea or dropped from the sky. Lituma started, speechless, opening his eyes wide. He wasn't dreaming: it was Colonel Mindreau.

"Good evening, Colonel." Lieutenant Silva jumped out of the boat in which he was sitting, dropping the guitar into the sand. Lituma saw his boss half reach for the pistol he always wore on his right hip.

"Please stay seated," said the colonel's shadow. "I was looking for you and I suspected the nocturnal guitar player I'd been hearing might be you."

"I was just seeing if I still remembered how to play. But I seem to have lost my touch. Lack of practice, I guess."

The shadow nodded. "You're a better detective than a guitar player."

"Thank you, Colonel."

"He's come to kill us." Lituma watched Colonel Mindreau step toward them, his face suddenly illuminated by the moonlight. Lituma could see his wide forehead, the two deep furrows on his brow, and his precise military mustache. Had he been this pale the two times he'd seen him in his office? Maybe it was the moon that made him seem so pale. His face was neither threatening nor angry, but indifferent. His voice had the same haughty tone it had that last time in his office. What now? Lituma felt an emptiness in his stomach: "This is what we were waiting for."

"Only a good detective could clear up the murder of that deserter so quickly. Barely two weeks. Right, Lieutenant?"

"Nineteen days, to be precise, Colonel."

Lituma never took his eyes off the colonel's hands, but they were not in the moonlight. Did he have his revolver out? Would he threaten the lieutenant, demanding he retract what he'd put in the report? Would he just shoot him two or three times? Would he shoot Lituma as well? Perhaps he'd come to arrest them. Maybe he had his MPs surrounding them while he distracted them with this gab. Lituma sharpened his ears and looked around. No one was coming, and except for the sea, there was no other noise. In front of him, Lituma had the old pier, which rose and fell with the waves. The sea gulls slept on the rusty ladder encrusted with shells and starfish that ran up and down the pier. The first order Lieutenant Silva had ever given Lituma was to chase off the kids who climbed up the ladder to ride the pier up and down on the waves.

"Nineteen days," echoed the colonel after a while.

He was speaking without irony, without rage, in glacial tones, as if nothing in all this mattered or affected him in the slightest. Deep in his voice there was an inflection, a pause, a way of accentuating certain syllables, that reminded Lituma of his daughter's voice. "The Unstoppables were right," he thought. "I'm no good at this stuff, I don't like being afraid."

"Not bad at all, especially when you think that it takes years to solve some of these crimes. Some are never solved."

Lieutenant Silva said nothing. There was a long silence in which none of the three men moved. The pier was seesawing violently. Could some kid be up there bouncing? Lituma heard the colonel's breathing, as well as his own and the lieutenant's. "I've never been so afraid in my life."

"Do you think you'll be rewarded with a promotion for this?" Lituma realized that, with only a short-sleeved shirt on, the colonel must be cold. He was a short man, at least half a head shorter than Lituma. In his day, there must not have been a minimum height requirement for the service academies.

"I don't come up for promotion until July of next year, Colonel." Now. Now his hand would rise and he'd start shooting: the lieutenant's head would splatter like a ripe papaya. But just then the colonel raised his right hand to wipe his mouth, and Lituma could see it was empty. So why had he come? "In answer to your question, sir, no, I don't think I'll be promoted for solving this case. Speaking frankly, I think this business is going to cause me a lot of headaches, Colonel."

"Are you so sure you've found the definitive solution?"

The shadow didn't move, and Lituma realized that the colonel spoke without parting his lips, like a ventriloquist.

"Only death is definitive," murmured the lieutenant. His posture and speech betrayed not the slightest apprehension, as if this conversation didn't concern him in any way, as if they were talking about other people. "He's playing along with the colonel," Lituma thought.

The lieutenant cleared his throat and went on: "Some details are still unclear, but I think the three key questions have been answered. Who killed Palomino Molero. How he was killed. Why he was killed."

Either the colonel had stepped back or the light had shifted: his face was again in darkness. The pier rose and fell. The cone of light from the lighthouse swept the water, turning it gold.

"I read the report you sent to your superiors. The Guardia Civil informed my superiors, and they were kind enough to send me a copy."

His expression hadn't changed; he spoke neither more quickly nor with more emotion than before. A gust of wind ruffled the colonel's sparse hair, which he immediately smoothed. Lituma remained tense and frightened, but now he had two extra images in his mind: the kid and Alicia Mindreau. The paralyzed girl watched in horror as they shoved the boy into a blue van. On the way to the rocky field, the airmen tried to please the officer by putting out their cigarettes on Palomino Molero's arms, neck, and face. When he screamed, they laughed, nudging each other. "Make him suffer, make him suffer," thundered Lieutenant Dufó. Then, kissing his fingers: "You'll be sorry you were ever born, that I promise you." He saw that Lieutenant Silva had moved away from the boat and was contemplating the sea, his hands in his pockets.

"Does this mean the matter will be covered up, Colonel?"

"I have no idea," replied the colonel dryly, as if the question were too banal or stupid, a waste of his precious time. But almost immediately he began to doubt: "I don't think so, not now anyway. It's hard, it would be . . . I just don't know. It depends on my superiors, not on me."

"The big guys again," thought Lituma. Why did the colonel talk as if none of this mattered to him? Why had he come if that was the case?

"I have to know one thing, Lieutenant." He paused, and Lituma thought he looked at him for an instant, as if only now he'd noticed him and had at the same time decided that he could go on talking in front of this nobody. "Did my daughter tell you I took advantage of her? Did she say that?"

Lituma watched Lieutenant Silva turn toward the colonel.

"She did suggest that . . ." he murmured, swallowing hard. "She wasn't explicit, she didn't actually say 'took advantage.' But she suggested that you . . . that she was a wife and not a daughter to you, Colonel."

Lieutenant Silva was nonplussed and tongue-tied. Lituma had never seen him so confused. He was sorry for him, for Colonel Mindreau, for the kid, for the girl. He was so sorry for the whole world he felt like crying, damn it. He realized he was trembling. Josefino had defined him to a T, he was a sentimental asshole and would always be one.

"Did she also tell you that I would kiss her feet? That after taking advantage of her I would get down on my knees and beg her to forgive me?" Colonel Mindreau wasn't really asking questions but confirming what he already seemed certain of.

Lieutenant Silva stuttered something Lituma couldn't understand. It might have been "I think so." Lituma wanted to run away. If only someone would come and interrupt this scene.

"Then I, mad with remorse, would hand her my revolver so she would kill me?" the colonel went on in a low voice. He was tired and seemed far away.

This time the lieutenant did not answer. There was a long pause. The colonel's silhouette was rigid and the old pier rose and fell, buffeted by the waves.

"Are you all right?"

"The English word for it is 'delusions,' " said the colonel firmly, as if speaking to no one in particular. "There is no word for it in Spanish. Because 'delusions' means illusions,

Who · Killed · Palomino · Molero?

fantasies, deception, and fraud. An illusion which is also a deception. A deceptive, fraudulent fantasy." He breathed deeply, as if hyperventilating, and then put his hand to his mouth. "To take Alicia to New York, I sold my parents' house. I spent my savings. I even mortgaged my pension. In the United States they cure every sickness there is, they work scientific miracles. Isn't that what they say? Well, if that was true, then any sacrifice would be worthwhile. I wanted to save my daughter and myself as well.

"They didn't cure her. But at least they discovered she had delusions. She'll never be cured, because it's something that never gets better. It just gets worse. It grows like a cancer, as long as the cause is there to stimulate it. The gringos explained it to me in their usual crude way. Her problem is you. You are the cause. She holds you responsible for the death of the mother she never knew. All the things she invents, these terrible things she makes up about you, the things she told the nuns at the Sacred Heart School in Lima, the things she told the nuns at the Lourdes School in Piura, that she told her aunts, and friends—that you beat her, that you're stingy, that you torment her, that you tie her to the bed and whip her. All to avenge her mother's death.

"But you haven't seen anything yet. Get ready for something much worse. Because later, when she grows up, she'll accuse you of having tried to kill her, of having raped her, of having had her raped. The most horrible things. And she won't even realize she's lying. Because she believes and lives her lies just as if they were the truth. Delusions. That's what they call it in English. We have no word for it in Spanish."

There was a long silence. The sea had become almost silent, too, just a low whisper. "I'm hearing a lot of words I've never heard before," thought Lituma.

"That may well be the case," he heard the lieutenant say in a severe and respectful tone. "But . . . the fantasy or madness of your daughter does not explain everything, if you don't mind my saying so." He paused, perhaps waiting for the colonel to say something or perhaps because he was searching for the right words. "I'm thinking about the way the boy was tortured."

Lituma closed his eyes. There he was: roasting under the implacable sun in the flinty wasteland, tortured from head to foot, surrounded by indifferent, browsing goats. Hung, burned with cigarettes, a stick shoved up his ass. Poor kid.

"That's another matter," said the colonel. "But," he corrected himself instantly, "you're right, it doesn't explain it."

"You asked me a question and I answered it. Now allow me to ask you a question. Was there any reason to torture the kid like that? I ask because frankly I just don't understand."

"Neither do I. Oh, I guess I do understand. Now. At first I didn't. He got drunk and got his men drunk. Liquor and a need for revenge turned him from a poor devil into a sadist. Need for revenge, a broken heart, tarnished honor. Those things exist even if a policeman doesn't understand them, Lieutenant. He seemed to be only a poor devil, not a sadist. A single bullet between the eyes would have been enough. And a discreet grave. Those were my orders. The stupid bloodbath, naturally, was not my idea. Now not even all that matters. It happened the way it happened and everyone has to take responsibility for what he does. I've always done that."

He gulped air again and panted. Lituma heard the lieutenant ask: "You were not there, then? Only Lieutenant Dufó and his men?

To Lituma it seemed that the colonel was hacking, as if he were about to spit. But he didn't.

"That was my consolation prize for him, the bullet that would soothe his wounded pride," he said coldly. "He surprised me. I didn't think him capable of things like that. His men also surprised me. They were Molero's buddies, after all. There is an element of bestiality in all of us. Educated or ignorant, all of us. I suppose there's more among the lower classes, the *cholos*. Resentment, complexes of all kinds. Liquor and praise from their superior did the rest. There was no need to go that far, of course. I'm not sorry about anything, if that's what you want to know. Have you ever heard of an airman who could kidnap and rape the daughter of a base commander and get away with it? But I would have done things more quickly and cleanly. A bullet in the back of the neck. End of story."

"He's just like his daughter," thought Lituma. "Elusions, delusions, whatever it is."

"Did Molero rape her, Colonel?" Once again, Lituma found that the lieutenant was asking the same questions he was thinking. "That he kidnapped her is a fact. Although it might be more accurate to say that they ran away together. They were in love and wanted to get married. The whole town of Amotape could testify to that. So where does the rape come in?"

Lituma again heard the colonel hacking. When he finally spoke, he was the same despotic, cutting man who'd spoken with them in his office: "The daughter of a base commander does not fall in love with a recruit," he told them, annoyed at having to explain something so obvious. "Colonel Mindreau's daughter does not fall in love with a guitar player from Castilla."

"She gets it from him," thought Lituma. From the father she supposedly hates so much, Alicia Mindreau inherits this mania for calling people *cholos* and treating them like dirt.

"I'm not making it up," he heard Lieutenant Silva say softly. "It was Miss Alicia who told us. We didn't have to ask her about it, Colonel. She said they loved each other and if the priest had been in Amotape they would have been married. A rape?"

"Haven't I explained all that already?" Colonel Mindreau raised his voice for the first time. "Delusions, delusions. Lying fantasies. She wasn't in love with him, she couldn't fall in love with him. Can't you see she was doing what she always does? Just what she did when she told you all those things. Just what she did when she went to the nuns at the Lourdes School to show them wounds she'd inflicted on herself, just so she could do me some harm. She was getting revenge, punishing me, making me pay for what hurt me the most, the death of her mother. As if"—he sighed and gasped for air—"that death wasn't cross enough for me to bear all my life. Can't a policeman's mind grasp all this?"

"No, motherfucker, it can't," thought Lituma. "It can't." Why make up rules like that? Why couldn't Alicia Min-

dreau fall in love with that skinny kid who played the
guitar so beautifully and sang with that tender, romantic
voice? Why was it impossible for a little white girl to be
in love with a little *cholo?* Why did the colonel see that
love as a tortuous conspiracy against him?

"I also explained it to Palomino Molero," he heard the
colonel say, again in that impersonal tone that distanced
him from them and from what he was saying. "Just as I've
explained it to you. In more detail to him. More clearly.
Without threats or orders. Not as a colonel to an airman,
but as one man to another. Giving him a chance to act
like a gentleman, to be what he wasn't."

He fell silent, and passed his hand rapidly over his mouth,
as if it were a flyswatter. Lituma, half closing his eyes, could
see them: the colonel, severe and neat, with his straight
mustache and his cold eyes, and the kid, standing at attention, stuffed into his recruit's uniform, probably brand-new
and with shiny buttons, his hair freshly cut. The colonel,
short and domineering, walking around his office as he
spoke, the sound of propellers and motors in the background; and the airman, very pale, not daring to move a
muscle, blink, open his mouth, even to breathe.

*That child, even though she talks, laughs, and does what
other girls do, is not like them. She's fragile, a crystal, a
flower, a defenseless dove* (Lituma realized that the colonel
was really saying: I could simply say to you that an airman
is forbidden even to look at the daughter of the base commander; a boy from Castilla cannot aspire, even in his
wildest dreams, to Alicia Mindreau. I want you to know
this and to know as well that you must not go near her, look

at her, even dream about her, or you'll pay for your daring with your life) *but instead of just forbidding him to see her, I explained it all to him, man to man. Believing that a guitar player from Castilla could still be a rational being, could think like a decent person. He told me he understood, that he had no idea Alicia was that way, that he would never look at her or speak to her again. And that night, the hypocritical cholo kidnapped her and took advantage of her. He thought he had me, the poor man. That's it, I raped her. Now you'll just have to resign yourself to our getting married. No, my boy, my daughter, this sick child, can do what she likes with me, can trick and disgrace me all she likes, and I have to carry this cross God has imposed on me. She can do that, and I . . . but not you, you poor fool.*

He fell silent, took a deep breath, and gasped. Then again the silence, regularly interrupted by the regular fall of the waves. The pier had stopped bouncing up and down. And once again Lituma heard his chief ask the question that was on the tip of his own tongue: "And why Ricardo Dufó? Why could he be Alicia Mindreau's boyfriend, her fiancé?"

"Ricardo Dufó is no beggar from Castilla. He's an officer. A man from a good family. But above all because he's got a weak character and a weak mind," shot back the colonel, fed up that no one but he could see what was plain as daylight. "Because, through that poor devil Ricardo Dufó, I could go on taking care of her, protecting her. Just as I had sworn to her dying mother I would. God and Mercedes know I've kept my word, despite what it's cost me."

His voice broke and he coughed several times, trying to

cover up an irrepressible anguish. Off in the distance, cats were howling and hissing in a frenzy: were they fighting or screwing? Everything in the world is confusing, damn it.

"But I haven't come about this and I'm not going to continue talking about my family with you," the colonel cut in sharply. He changed voices again, softening his tone: "I don't want to waste your time, Lieutenant."

"I don't even exist for him," thought Lituma. It was better that way. He felt safe knowing he'd been forgotten, abolished, by the colonel. There was an interminable pause in which the colonel seemed to be desperately fighting against his own loss of speech, trying to pronounce some rebellious and fugitive words.

"You're not wasting my time, Colonel."

"I'd appreciate it if you wouldn't mention this matter in your report," he finally blurted out with difficulty.

"You mean about your daughter? About her hinting that you'd taken advantage of her?"

"I'd appreciate it if you didn't mention it in your report," he repeated in a surer voice. He passed his hand over his mouth and added, "Not for my sake, but for hers. This would have been a banquet for the newspapers. I can just see the headlines, all that journalistic pus and poison raining down on us." He coughed, gasped, and made an effort to seem calm before he murmured: "A minor has to be protected from scandal. At any price."

"I have to inform you, Colonel," Lituma heard the lieutenant say, "that I didn't mention the matter because it was so vague, and also because it wasn't relevant to Palomino Molero's murder. But don't think that's the end of it. When the affair becomes public, if it does, everything will depend on what your daughter says. She'll be harassed, pursued day and night by people trying to get her to make statements. And the dirtier and more scandalous they are, the more they'll exploit them. You know it. If it's as you say, if she suffers from hallucinations, delusions—is that what they're called?—it would be better to put her in a sanatorium, or send her abroad. Pardon me for sticking my nose into your personal life."

He stopped talking because the colonel's shadow had made an impatient gesture.

"Since I didn't know if I'd find you, I left you a note at the station, under the door," he said, ending the conversation.

"Understood, Colonel."

"Good night," the colonel said in his cutting voice.

But he didn't leave. Lituma watched him turn around, take a few steps toward the shore, stop, his face toward the sea, and stand stock-still. The beacon from the lighthouse momentarily revealed the short, imperious figure dressed in khaki. Lituma and Lieutenant Silva exchanged indecisive looks. Finally the lieutenant signaled that they should leave.

They walked away without saying a word, the sand muffling their footsteps. They left the colonel and wended their way through the boats toward Talara. When they reached the town, Lituma turned to look back at the beach. The colonel's figure, a shadow lighter than the shadows around it, stood in the same spot. Out at sea, there were twinkling yellow lights scattered along the horizon. Which of those lanterns was hanging on Don Matías's boat?

Talara was deserted. There were no lights shining in the small wooden houses. Lituma had many things to ask about and comment on, but he didn't dare open his mouth, paralyzed as he was by an ambiguous sensation of confusion and sadness. Could what the colonel told them be the truth? Maybe it was. That's why he'd thought the girl had seemed nutty; he wasn't wrong. At times he watched Lieutenant Silva out of the corner of his eye: he had the guitar on his shoulder, as if it were a rifle or a hoe, and seemed pensive, distant. How could he see with those sunglasses on?

When the shot went off, Lituma jumped. At the same time, it was as if he'd been expecting it. It broke the silence, briefly and brutally, and made a dull echo. Now everything was quiet and mute again. He stood still and looked at the lieutenant. After stopping for a moment, he began walking once more.

"But, Lieutenant," said Lituma, trotting to catch up, "didn't you hear?"

The officer was walking even more quickly now.

"Hear what, Lituma?"

"The shot, Lieutenant. Over on the beach. Didn't you hear it?"

"I heard a noise that might have been a thousand things, Lituma. A drunk farting, a whale burping. A thousand things. I have no proof that noise was a shot."

Lituma's heart pounded. He was sweating and his shirt clung to his back. He was walking next to the lieutenant, shocked, stumbling, not understanding a thing.

"Aren't we going to see about him?" Lituma asked, suddenly feeling dizzy.

"To see what about him, Lituma?"

"To see if Colonel Mindreau killed himself, Lieutenant. Wasn't that the shot we just heard?"

"We'll find out soon enough, Lituma. Whether it was or not, we'll find out soon enough. What's your hurry? Wait until someone comes, some fisherman, a bum, someone'll find him and tell us. If it's true that gentleman killed himself, as you seem to think. Better yet, wait until we're back at the station. It may be that the mystery that's tormenting you will be cleared up there. Didn't you hear the colonel say he'd left us a note?"

"So you think that note will be his testament, Lieutenant? That he came looking for us knowing that after he talked to us he was going to kill himself?"

"Damn but you're slow, boy," said the lieutenant, sighing. He patted Lituma on the arm to raise his spirits. "Well, you're going to have to go through a lot, but soon you'll understand how things work. See what I mean, Lituma?"

They said nothing more until they reached the station, a run-down little house with peeling paint. A cloud hid the moon, and the lieutenant had to light a match to find the lock, and he had to twist the key around a lot, as usual, before it yielded. Lighting another match, he searched the floor, beginning at the threshold and working his way in, until the match burned his fingers and he had to blow it out, cursing. Lituma ran to light the paraffin lamp, which he did so awkwardly it seemed to take an age. The little flame finally caught on: a red tongue with a blue center that flickered before blazing up.

The envelope had slipped between two floorboards, and Lituma watched the lieutenant hunker down and carefully pick it up as if it were a fragile and precious object. He already knew the motions the lieutenant would make and in fact did make: he pushed his cap back on his head,

took off his sunglasses, and sat down on a corner of the desk
with his legs spread wide. Then he very carefully tore open
the envelope and used two fingers to pull out a small, almost
transparent white paper. Lituma could make out the lines
of even writing that covered the entire page. He brought
over the lamp so his boss could read more easily. Filled with
anxiety, he saw the lieutenant's eyes move slowly from left
to right and back again, and his face slowly twisted into an
expression of disgust or perplexity, or perhaps both things.

"Well, Lieutenant?"

"Holy shit," he said, letting the hand holding the white
paper drop down to his knee.

"Did he kill himself? Will you let me read it, Lieutenant?"

"That son of a bitch takes the cake." Lieutenant Silva
handed him the letter. As he read, believing and not believing, understanding and not understanding, he heard
the lieutenant add: "He not only killed himself, Lituma.
The son of a bitch killed the girl, too."

Lituma raised his head and stared at the lieutenant, not
knowing what to say or do. He had the lamp in his left
hand, so those shadows jumping on the walls meant that
he was trembling. A grimace deformed the lieutenant's
face, and Lituma saw him blink and squint, as if the glare
were blinding him.

"What do we do now?" he stuttered, feeling somehow
guilty of something. "Go to the base, to the colonel's house,
to find out if he really killed the girl?"

"Do you think there's any way he didn't, Lituma?"

"I don't know. I mean, I think he did kill her. That's
why he was behaving so strangely out on the beach. I also

think he killed himself—that was the shot we heard. Son of a bitch."

"You're right," said Lieutenant Silva. "Son of a bitch."

For a moment they were silent, immobile, standing among the shadows that danced along the walls, on the floor, over the furniture of the dilapidated office.

"What do we do now, Lieutenant?"

"Well, I don't know what you're going to do," he said brusquely, standing up as if he'd suddenly remembered he had something urgent to attend to. He seemed possessed of a violent energy. "But for the moment I'd advise you to do nothing except get some sleep. Until someone comes to tell us about the two deaths."

Lituma watched him stride purposefully out of the room toward the shadows on the street, making his usual gestures: settling the holster he always wore on his belt and putting on his sunglasses.

"And where are you off to, Lieutenant?" he muttered, shocked and already sure of what he was going to hear.

"I'm gonna screw that fat bitch once and for all."

8

DOÑA ADRIANA laughed again, and Lituma realized that while all Talara was gossiping, weeping, or speculating about the momentous events which had taken place, she did nothing but laugh. This had been going on for three days. That's how she'd greeted them and bidden them farewell at breakfast, lunch, and supper—the purest horse-laugh. By contrast, Lieutenant Silva was cranky and out of sorts, as if he'd eaten something that had disagreed with him. For the fifteenth time in three days, Lituma wondered what the hell had gone on between them. Father Domingo's bells echoed through the town, calling the faithful to Mass. Still laughing, Doña Adriana crossed herself.

"What do you think they'll do to this Lieutenant Dufó?" rasped Don Jerónimo.

It was lunchtime, and along with Don Jerónimo, Lieutenant Silva, and Lituma, there was a young couple who had come from Zorritos for a baptism.

"He'll be tried in a military court," an ill-humored Lieutenant Silva replied, without raising his eyes from his half-empty plate.

"But they'll have to convict him of something, don't you think?" Don Jerónimo was eating hash and white rice, fanning himself with a newspaper. He chewed with his mouth open and sprayed food particles all around him. "After all, if a guy does what they say this Dufó did to Palomino Molero, you just don't let him go free, right, Lieutenant?"

"Right, right, you just can't let him go free," agreed the lieutenant, his mouth full and his face radiating his disgust at not being left in peace at lunch. "They'll do something to him, at least I imagine they will."

Doña Adriana laughed again, and Lituma felt the lieutenant tense up and sink into his seat as she approached them. He must be on edge: he's not even chasing away the flies buzzing around his face. She was wearing a flowered dress, very low-cut, and as she walked she shook her hips and breasts vigorously. She looked healthy, happy, and at peace with the world.

"Have another glass of water, Lieutenant, and don't eat so quickly. You might swallow down the wrong pipe," said Doña Adriana, laughing, as she patted him on the back in a way even more mocking than the words she spoke.

"You've been in a good mood lately," said Lituma, staring at her without recognizing her. She was a different person, a coquette, what had gotten into her?

"There must be a reason," said Doña Adriana, picking up the plates from the table where the couple from Zorritos were sitting, and heading for the kitchen. She wiggled her backside as if waving goodbye to them. "Holy Jesus," thought Lituma.

"Do you have any idea why she's been like this, so bubbly, for the last three days, Lieutenant?"

Instead of answering, the lieutenant pierced him with a

homicidal look from behind his dark glasses and went back to contemplating the street. There a vulture was furiously pecking at something. Then, suddenly, it flapped its wings and flew away.

"Want me to tell you something, Lieutenant?" said Don Jerónimo. "I hope you won't get mad."

"If it'll make me mad, it might be better not to say it," growled the lieutenant. "I'm not in the mood for bullshit."

"Over and out," growled back the taxi driver.

"Will there be more killings?" asked Doña Adriana from the kitchen, laughing.

"She's vamping us," Lituma said to himself. "I have to pay a visit to Liau's chicks. I'm getting rusty." The taxi driver's table was on the other side of the room, so in order to talk to the lieutenant he had to shout over the heads of the couple from Zorritos, who had been following the conversation with growing interest.

"Well, even if you do get mad, I am going to say something to you," decided Don Jerónimo, slapping the table with his newspaper. "There's not a soul in Talara, man, woman, child, or dog, who believes that story. Not even that vulture out there could swallow it."

The vulture had returned and was sitting there, black and mean, chewing on a lizard it had in its beak. The lieutenant went on eating, indifferent, concentrating on his own thoughts and bad mood.

"And what is 'that story' if you don't mind telling us, Don Jerónimo?"

"That Colonel Mindreau killed his daughter and then killed himself," said the taxi driver, spewing food. "Who'd be dumb enough to believe that?"

"Me," said Lituma. "I'm dumb enough to believe that the colonel killed her and then committed suicide."

"Don't play dumb with me, Officer Lituma. The two of them were bumped off so they wouldn't talk. So the murder of Palomino Molero could be blamed on Mindreau. Who do you think you're kidding?"

"Is that really what people are saying now?" Lieutenant Silva raised his head from his plate. "That Colonel Mindreau was bumped off? And who's supposed to have killed him?"

"The big guys, of course. Who else? Don't kid me, Lieutenant. Come on, we're all friends here. The fact is you can't talk. Everybody says they've shut you up and won't let you get to the bottom of the case. The usual stuff."

The lieutenant shrugged his shoulders, as if all this chatter meant nothing to him.

"People are actually saying he took advantage of his daughter," said Don Jerónimo through a shower of rice. "What pigs. Poor man. Don't you think so, Adrianita?"

"I think lots of things, ha-ha-ha!"

"So people think this is all a made-up story," murmured the lieutenant, turning back to his lunch with a bitter grimace.

"Of course. To protect the real guilty parties, what else could it be?"

The I.P.C.'s siren wailed, and the vulture raised its head and hunched down. It remained like that for a few seconds, tense and waiting. Then it hopped off.

"So what reason do people give for the murder of Palomino Molero?" asked Lituma.

"Smuggling. Worth millions," declared Don Jerónimo.

"First they killed the kid because he found out something. And when Colonel Mindreau discovered what was going on, or was about to discover it, they killed him and the girl. And since they know what people like to hear, they invented that filthy stuff about how he killed Molero because he was jealous, that Molero had something going with his daughter, who he was supposed to have abused. The smoke screen was a success. Nobody's talking about the important thing: the money."

"Damn but they have terrific imaginations," said the lieutenant, sighing. He was scraping his fork along the plate as if he wanted to break it.

"Don't swear or your tongue will fall right out," said Doña Adriana, laughing. She stood right next to the lieutenant with a saucer of mango pudding, and when she put it in front of him, she came so close that her ample hip rubbed the lieutenant's arm. He pulled it back instantly. "Ha-ha-ha!"

"Nice table manners," thought Lituma. "What the hell's going on with Doña Adriana." Not only was she making fun of the lieutenant, but she was flirting with him like crazy. But he did nothing. He seemed inhibited, demoralized, unable to deal with Doña Adriana's wisecracks and jokes. He, too, seemed like a different person. Any other time, those little moves by Doña Adriana would have made him happy as a lark and he would have followed her lead. Now nothing could stir him out of the gloom which had made him seem like a sick dog for the last three days. "What the fuck happened that night?"

"In Zorritos, people have been talking about that smuggling thing," offered the man. He was young, had his hair slicked back, and had a gold tooth. He wore a pink shirt, stiff with starch, and he spoke too rapidly. He looked over at the woman who must have been his wife: "Isn't that right, Marisita?"

"Yes, Panchito, that's right. Absolutely right."

"It seems they were bringing in refrigerators and stoves. To pull off a deal like that, you've got to be talking millions."

"I'm sorry about Alicita Mindreau," said Marisita, pouting as if she were about to cry. "The girl is the innocent victim in this business. Poor child. What crimes people commit. What makes me mad is that the real guilty parties always get away. Nothing ever happens to them, right, Pancho?"

"Around here, it's always us poor people who get shafted," complained Don Jerónimo. "Never the big guys. Right, Lieutenant?"

The lieutenant got up so violently that his table and chair almost fell over.

"I'm getting out of here," he announced, sick of everything and everyone. "Lituma, are you going to stick around?"

"I'll be right with you, Lieutenant. Just let me drink my coffee."

"Enjoy yourself." Doña Adriana's mocking farewells followed him right out the door.

A few minutes later, when Doña Adriana brought Lituma his coffee, she sat down in the lieutenant's chair.

"I'm so curious I just can't take it anymore. Aren't you going to tell me what happened the other night between you and the lieutenant?"

"Ask him," she replied, her round face blazing with malice.

"I have asked him, at least ten times. But he just plays dumb. Come on, don't be like that, tell me what happened."

"Only women are supposed to be that curious, Lituma."

"Some people are saying it might have more to do with espionage than with smuggling," he heard Don Jerónimo say to the couple from Zorritos. "The man who said it was Don Teotonio Calle Frías, the owner of the movie house and a serious man who just doesn't go around shooting his mouth off."

"If he says it, there must be something to it," added Panchito.

"Where there's smoke, there's fire," recited Marisa.

"Look, Doña Adrianita, don't get mad because I'm asking. I have to because I'm dying of curiosity. Did you go to bed with the lieutenant? Did you give in at last?"

"How dare you ask me a question like that, you pig." Admonishing him with her raised index finger, she pretended to be angry. The same sardonic, self-satisfied gleam was still in her dark eyes, and her mouth was still shaped into the ambiguous smile of a person who's remembering a bad deed, half sorry and half glad to have done it. "Anyway, keep your voice down. Matías might hear."

"Palomino Molero found out that military secrets were being sent to Ecuador and they killed him," said Don Jerónimo. "The head of the spy ring was none other than Colonel Mindreau himself."

"The plot thickens," said the Zorritos man. "It's like a movie."

"Exactly, like a movie."

"How's he going to hear if he's in there snoring away. It's just that everything's been so strange since that night. I've been trying to guess what happened here to make you so merry and the lieutenant so down."

Doña Adriana laughed so hard that tears filled her eyes. Her body shook, and her huge breasts danced up and down hanging free under her flowered dress.

"Of course he's down. I think I've cooled him off forever, Lituma. Your boss's days as a Don Juan are finished. Ha-ha-ha!"

"I'm not surprised at what Don Teotonio Frías is saying," said the Zorritos man, licking his gold tooth. "From the start, I suspected that with all these murders there had to be Ecuadoreans in the woodpile."

"But what did you do to cool him off, Doña Adriana? How'd you flatten him like that? Come on, tell me."

"Besides, they probably raped the Mindreau girl before they killed her," said the lady from Zorritos, sighing. "That's what they always do. From those monkeys you can expect anything. And I say that even though I have relatives in Ecuador."

"He stormed into my bedroom with his pistol in his hand, trying to scare me." She held in her laughter and half closed her eyes so she could see once again the scene that amused her so much. "I was asleep and he frightened me out of my wits. I first thought it was a thief, but it was your boss. He smashed right through the lock, the shameless fool. Thought he'd scare me. Poor, poor guy."

"I haven't heard anything about that," muttered Don Jerónimo, sticking his head out from behind the newspaper he shooed flies with. "But, of course, it wouldn't surprise me that besides killing her they'd rape her. A bunch of them, probably."

"He began by telling me a bunch of silly things," whispered Doña Adriana.

"For instance?"

I can't go on living this way. I'm drowning in my desire for you. This desire I feel is killing me, I've reached my limit. If I don't have you, I'll end up blowing my brains out. Or maybe I'll kill you.

"What a riot." Lituma was twisted up with laughter. "Did he really say he was drowning in desire for you and then blame you for treating him badly?"

"He thought he'd either make me sorry for him or scared of him, or both. But he was the one who got the surprise."

"Certainly, certainly," said the man from Zorritos. "A bunch of them. That's always the way it is."

"What did you do, Doña Adrianita?"

"I took off my nightgown and lay there naked," she whispered, blushing. Just like that: she took it off and was stark naked. She made a lightning-quick move with both arms, ripping off the gown and throwing it from the bed. Her face, framed by her tangled hair, and her pudgy body in the moonlight radiated nothing but anger and disdain.

"Naked?" Lituma blinked three times.

"I said some things to your boss he never dreamed he'd hear. Filth."

"Filth?" Lituma blinked again, all ears.

Here I am, why don't you strip, cholito. Doña Adriana went on, her voice vibrating with indignation. She thrust forward her breasts and her stomach and held her hands at her waist. *Or are you ashamed to show it to me? Is it that small, daddy? Come on, hurry up, take off your pants and show it to me. Come on, take me right now. Show me what a man you really are, baby. Give it to me five times in a row, that's what my husband does every night. He's old and you're young, so you can break his record easily, right? Give it to me, six or seven times. Can you do it?*

"Did you really say those things," stammered Lituma, shocked out of his wits.

But, but . . . stammered the lieutenant. *What's gotten into you, Doña Adriana?*

"I didn't recognize myself either, Lituma. I have no idea where I got all that dirty stuff. But I thank Our Lord in Captivity over in Ayabaca for giving me the inspiration. I made a pilgrimage there once, on foot, all the way to Ayabaca, during His festival in October. That's why I got that idea just then. The poor man was as shocked as you are. *Go on, baby, take off your pants. Let me see your dick. I want to see how big it is and to count how many times you'll come. Think you'll reach eight?*"

"But, but . . ." stuttered Lituma, his face burning, his eyes as wide as saucers.

You have no right to make fun of me like that, stuttered the lieutenant, his mouth hanging open.

"Because I said all that in the calmest voice you ever heard, Lituma. I was so mad and made such fun of him that I won the moral victory. He was totally destroyed. You should have seen him."

"I'm not surprised, Doña Adriana, who wouldn't be? I'm destroyed just listening. What did he do then?"

"Of course he didn't take off his pants or anything else.

Whatever lust he had when he came in evaporated just like that."

I didn't come here to be made fun of, shouted the lieutenant, not knowing how he was going to get out.

"*Of course not, you son of a bitch. You came here to scare me with your gun and to rape me, so you could feel you were a real man. Well, go ahead and rape me, Superman. Go on, get busy. Rape me ten times in a row, daddy. I'll be satisfied. What are you waiting for?*"

"You went crazy."

"Yes, I did go crazy. But it worked. Your boss took off like a shot with his tail between his legs. And he made out that it was I who offended him, the wise guy!"

I came here to confess my sincere feelings, and you do nothing but mock and insult me, protested the lieutenant. *Talking like a common whore to boot.*

"Look at him now. No spirit left. I'm almost sorry for him."

She laughed heartily again. Lituma was imbued with a sense of solidarity and sympathy for the lieutenant. That's why he was so depressed, his manhood, his masculine dignity had been humiliated. When he told the Unstoppables, they'd go crazy. They'd say that Doña Adriana and not La Chunga would be the next Queen of the Unstoppables and they'd sing their theme song in her honor.

"Some other people have said that it might have something to do with queers," insinuated the Zorritos man.

"Queers? Is that right?" Don Jerónimo blinked and licked his lips. "Might well, might well."

"It might indeed. You know that there are lots of queers in the service, and where there's queers, there's usually crime. Excuse us for talking like this in front of you, Marisita."

"There's nothing wrong, Panchito. That's the way life is."

"It might well," reflected Don Jerónimo. "But who with who? How do you figure it?"

"No one believes the story about Colonel Mindreau's committing suicide," Doña Adriana abruptly changed the subject.

"So I see," muttered Lituma.

"Neither do I, as a matter of fact. How could it be?"

"So you don't believe it either?" Lituma got up and signed the voucher for lunch. "But I believe the story you told me. And it's much more fantastic than the suicide of Colonel Mindreau. See you later, Doña Adriana."

"Listen, Lituma," she called him back. Her eyes radiated mischief and she lowered her voice. "Tell the lieutenant that tonight I'll make him something special so he'll love me again—just a little."

She giggled coquettishly, and Lituma laughed with her.

"I'll relay your message exactly as you said it, Doña Adriana. Bye."

Damn, who can understand women? He was walking toward the door when he heard Don Jerónimo behind him: "Lituma, old pal, why don't you tell us how much the big guys paid the lieutenant to make up that story about the colonel's suicide?"

"If that's your idea of a joke, I don't think it's very funny. And I don't think the lieutenant would either. If he were to find out, it might cost you, Don Jerónimo."

He heard the old taxi driver mutter, "Fucking cop," and

for an instant he considered going back. He didn't. He went
out into the oppressive afternoon heat, and walked along
the burning sand path, cutting through a horde of kids
kicking a rag ball. He started to sweat, and his shirt stuck
to his body. What Doña Adriana told him was incredible.
Could it be true? It had to be. Now he understood why the
lieutenant had been so downcast ever since that night.
When it came to that, the lieutenant himself was a case.
To want to screw Chubby just then, in the thick of a
tragedy. How could he do it? But it really went badly for
him. Doña Adriana had turned out to be a hell of a woman.
He imagined her naked, mocking the lieutenant, her robust
body shaking, and the lieutenant bewildered, not wanting
to believe what he was hearing and seeing. Who wouldn't
have thrown in the towel and run for it? He started to
laugh again.

At the station he found the lieutenant, bare-chested,
sitting at his desk, covered with sweat. He fanned himself
with one hand and with the other he held a telegram
right up to his sunglasses. Despite the dark glasses, Lituma
could make out the lieutenant's eyes as they followed the
lines of the message.

"The screwy thing about all this is that nobody believes
Colonel Mindreau killed the girl and himself. They're saying the dumbest damn things you ever heard, Lieutenant.
That it had to do with contraband, that it was a spy story,
that Ecuador was involved. Someone even suggested there
were fags in on it. Have you ever heard anything so stupid?"

"Bad news for you. You've been transferred to a little
station as imaginary as those stories, somewhere in Junín

Province. You've got to get there right away. They'll pay for the bus ticket."

"Junín?"

"I'm being transferred, too, but I still don't know where. Maybe the same place."

"That's got to be far away."

"Now you see, asshole," the lieutenant teased him affectionately. "You were so eager to solve the mystery of Palomino Molero. Well, now it's solved, and I did it for you. So what do we get for our trouble? You're transferred to the mountains, far from your heat and your people. They'll probably find a worse hole for me. That's how they thank you for a job well done in the Guardia Civil. What will become of you out there, Lituma? Your kind of animal just doesn't grow there. I feel sorry just thinking about how cold you're going to be."

"Sons of bitches."

About the Author

One of the world's finest writers, **Mario Vargas Llosa** was born in Peru in 1936. He has received virtually every important international literary prize, including the Ritz Paris Hemingway Award for *The War of the End of the World* (1984). His other works include *The Cubs and Other Stories* (1959), *Aunt Julia and the Scriptwriter* (1982), *Conversation in the Cathedral* (1983), *The Real Life of Alejandro Mayta* (1985), and *The Perpetual Orgy: Flaubert and Madame Bovary* (1987). After living in Paris, he returned to Peru in 1980, shortly before the restoration of democratic rule.

COLLIER FICTION

Beattie, Ann. *Where You'll Find Me.*
$7.95 ISBN 0-02-016560-9

Carrère, Emmanuel. *The Mustache.*
$7.95 ISBN 0-02-018870-6

Coover, Robert. *A Night at the Movies.*
$7.95 ISBN 0-02-019120-0

Dickinson, Charles. *With or Without.*
$7.95 ISBN 0-02-019560-5

Handke, Peter. *Across.*
$6.95 ISBN 0-02-051540-5

Handke, Peter. *Slow Homecoming.*
$8.95 ISBN 0-02-051530-8

Hemingway, Ernest. *The Garden of Eden.*
$8.95 ISBN 0-684-18871-6

Olson, Toby. *The Woman Who Escaped from Shame.*
$7.95 ISBN 0-02-023231-4

Pelletier, Cathie. *The Funeral Makers.*
$6.95 ISBN 0-02-023610-7

Phillips, Caryl. *A State of Independence.*
$6.95 ISBN 0-02-015080-6

Rush, Norman. *Whites.*
$6.95 ISBN 0-02-023841-X

Vargas Llosa, Mario. *Who Killed Palomino Molero?*
$6.95 ISBN 0-02-022570-9

West, Paul. *Rat Man of Paris.*
$6.95 ISBN 0-02-026250-7

Available at your local bookstore, or from
Macmillan Publishing Company, 100K Brown Street
Riverside, New Jersey 08370